I0756035

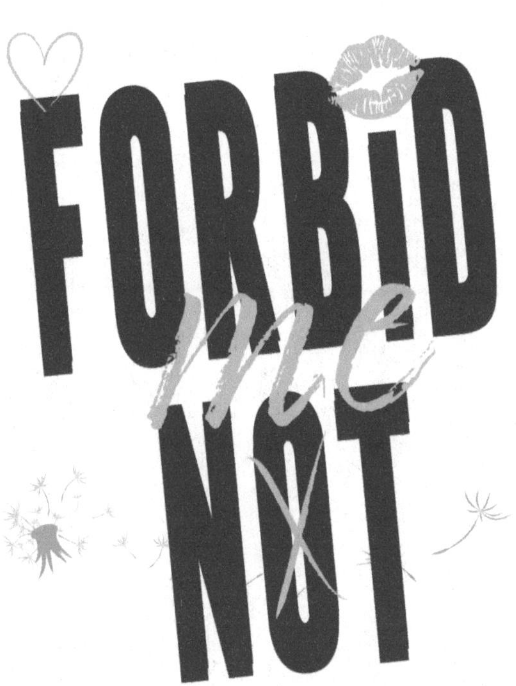
FORBID
me
NOT

FORBID *me* NOT

USA TODAY BESTSELLING AUTHOR

DV FISCHER

LNP

Forbid Me Not
Paperback Edition

Love N. Books Press
An Imprint of Wolfpack Publishing
1707 E. Diana Street
Tampa, FL 33610

www.lovenbookspress.com

Edited by My Brother's Editor
Cover Design by Rachel Chaya Designs

Paperback ISBN 979-8-89567-645-5
Ebook ISBN 979-8-89567-644-8
LCCN 2026933699

PLAYLIST

Slow Hands by Niall Horan
Body Like a Backroad by Sam Hunt
Do I want to know? by Arctic Monkeys
Young Blood by 5 Seconds of Summer
A Thousand Years by Christina Perri

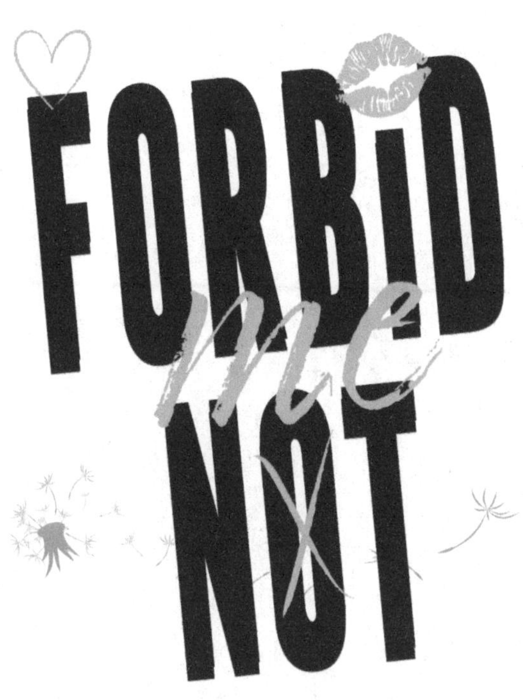
FORBID
me
NOT

CHAPTER 1
AVERY MOORE

I BOB my head as music blares from the speakers that my brother has set up throughout his two-bedroom campus apartment. The bass pounds against my body, so much so that the contents of my drink are having a hard time staying inside the red solo cup. Having been filled too full by my brother's friend, Jacob, it's splashing against the edge of my hand, and as drunk as I am, I lick it away like a cat sipping from a bowl of milk.

At this point, I really don't give a crap how weird I look because lord knows that literally no one is paying attention to me. As a bigger girl, I'm unnoticeable like that.

I survey the crowded living room as I close my mouth around a particularly juicy drop on the side of my cup. Hell, maybe even the licking will turn some guy on and he'll approach me and…

Gosh, it's only been a few months, and I've turned into a hussy. I wrinkle my nose in disgust.

It doesn't matter. There are far too many pretty girls here to flirt with. However, if one decided to give me the chance, I wouldn't say no to a little "attention."

Sucking my tongue back into my mouth, I frown. *No, Avery.* No having sex with a stranger. That's unlike you. You're a strong, confident woman.

Ugh, but I'm positive my vibrator is losing steam despite the new batteries I put in a week ago.

I glare at the drink because glaring at my greedy pussy would probably be more frowned upon than the licking of my own hand. "This is your fault," I slur to the drink and then quickly take a sip.

Someone loaded the jungle juice with a heavy hand, but I'm long past tasting and cringing at the amount of alcohol anymore. It tastes delicious.

I've been standing alone for…what…five minutes? Or has it been longer? Hell if I know. I have no idea where I set my phone so I can check for the time, and in this tight dress, there are no pockets. I don't even know where my heels are.

My best friend Ivy was standing next to me. But when she's drunk, she has the attention span of a fly and often disappears, the social butterfly that she is.

I didn't want to come to this party, but my brother begged me. He threw it for me so that he could introduce me, his sister and newbie to the college, to his friends, most particularly his best friend, whom I still haven't met. And though I haven't met all of them in this room, a great number came to introduce themselves in the beginning. You know, before all the alcohol. A few couldn't stop staring at my chest, and at the time, I cared. Big girl boobs and all that. But now? I definitely don't. Come stare at my breasts, boys! I really need to get laid.

No, I don't.

Yes, I do.

Crap.

But, as the popular guy's sister, I might as well have a paper bag over my face that says "Off limits" anyway because, though they looked at my boobs, they kept the conversation strictly friendly.

In a desperate attempt to not seem like a loser standing by herself, I look around to find Ivy so that she can talk me out of dry humping the nearest male, but when I spot her, she's on the couch with her lips locked to my brother's.

My shoulders slump. Well, isn't that just great?

Maybe I can pull her away. My brother gets her all the time, and I'm in serious need of a talking to right now.

As I make my way over to the couch to do just that, the music changes.

Whipping around, I gasp while wobbling unsteadily to the side. The press of bodies steadies me as my favorite song starts blaring. *Young Blood* pours into my soul, and immediately, I start dancing. It's far too crowded in the living room, however, so to get some space, I climb onto the coffee table and do a little twirl before rocking my hips. A few hoots and hollers come my way, making me grin as I continue to shake my body to the tune.

I'm not normally this brazen. I swear.

"Get it, Avery!" someone shouts.

I raise my hands in the air and sway them, briefly wondering what the hell I did with my drink.

As I do a spin, my foot slides off the table, and my eyes widen as I start to fall off the surface. It feels like slow motion as I fall, and I know, without a doubt, that it's going to be painful come morning.

Strong arms wrap around my waist before I can plummet to my death, holding on tight. Taking a few gasping breaths, I say *thank you* before looking up into the eyes of my savior. And the words die from my lips because staring back at me are the most gorgeous hazel eyes I've ever seen. There are flecks of gold in them, and around the outside of the iris is a rim of chocolate brown.

I don't know how long I stare at him because, again, time moves differently when you're wasted, but eventually, his full, red lips curve into a smile that accentuates a perfect jawline and the most beautiful nose I've ever seen. Can noses be beautiful? Heck yeah, they can.

"Are you okay?" he asks as the music switches to a new song. My cheeks immediately combust in flames. I definitely stared too long, and I probably looked like an idiot while doing so.

I wasn't introduced to this guy. I would have remembered. Definitely. No one forgets a face like that. And his smell…he smells like he dips himself in pheromones with a mix of body wash.

Slowly, he rights me, and burning with embarrassment, I turn to face him, taking him all in. He's wearing this year's Smithson University T-shirt, which clings to his body, revealing the tight and corded muscles in his arms and chest. He's taller than me, forcing me to look up to take in his hair. It's dark and styled messily, and if it doesn't make me swoon…

Remembering that he asked me a question, I tuck my curled, brown hair behind my ear and nod while glancing down at my bare feet. I curl my toes into the carpet as I answer, "Yes. Um. Yeah, I'm fine. Thank you."

"What's your name?" he calls over the music.

I flick my gaze back to him. He's studying my face, lingering on my rosy cheeks and my bottom lip tucked between my teeth. God, he has to know what kind of effect he has on me. And I don't know what possesses me, but I decide to lie about who I am. "Sarah," I answer.

Seriously. What is wrong with me? But it's too late to take it back.

Maybe I did it on purpose. Maybe I don't want to be known as the popular guy's sister. All the other guys seem to think I'm off limits, and I really don't want this guy to.

I'm too drunk to ponder on it long, however, because a grin spreads across his face, revealing straight, white teeth.

He's far too beautiful for his own good, and I think he knows it.

"Do you go to school here, or do you know someone and got invited?"

"Uh." I glance around. "Both?"

"Is that a question?" he asks, bending closer to my ear because, I swear, the music just amped up in volume.

"Um."

His lips press closer to my ear, his breath feathering my earlobe. "I'm just teasing you, Sarah."

A shiver overcomes my body, and he chuckles. At that moment, someone bumps into my back, forcing me forward and into his chest. He catches me before I nearly tip sideways, his hands going to my curvy waist. If I wasn't drunk, I'd be self-conscious about being touched there. Me and my weight have some issues that I'll probably never work out.

Instead of stiffening in his embrace, I sort of, um, melt against him, hands on his chest, head tucked under his chin. God, what am I doing?

My heart beats rapidly as his hands slide higher. I tip my head back to peer at his face, and he looks down at me as I whisper, "Sorry."

"It's okay," he murmurs back, eyes searching mine.

Something passes between us. A silent, drunken conversation that I've literally never had before but, I swear to God, it's the best feeling in the world. It kicks up the long-dead butterflies in my stomach, and before I know what I'm doing, I lift myself on my toes and press my lips to his perfect ones.

I expect him to endure it for a moment. I expect him to gently peel me off of him because, let's face it, there are far more skinnier and good-looking girls here besides me. But he doesn't. He...he kisses me back. My heartbeat sores into my ears, and the party fades away as we stand there, lips locked, hands beginning to roam each other's backs.

His lips slide over mine, and when his hand reaches up and cups my jaw, I moan into his mouth. It's a simple gesture, but I've never been kissed this way. Not by *the bastard*, and not by anyone before him.

He chuckles against my mouth, and it's honestly the sexiest thing I've ever heard. And then his tongue is teasing my bottom lip, and I open up for him. Our tongues dive into each other's mouths and holy shit. Despite the taste of jungle juice, he tastes just as good as he smells.

I grip the back of his shirt, leaning into the kiss. My lips and tongue move faster of their own accord, but he doesn't mind. He responds in kind, his other hand exploring my backside.

When I'm out of breath, I break the kiss. And boldly—because alcohol makes me strong—I ask, "Want to get out of here?"

My pussy literally clenches as I wait for his answer.

I don't have to wait long before he nods. But then, he says with a frown, "I don't live anywhere near here, and my friend would kill me if I drove right now."

Grinning, I grab his hand. "I live right across the hall." It's like it was meant to be.

He glances around once—for what, I don't know, but I don't wait to find out. By the hand, I drag him across the living room, moving between the people, and into the kitchen where the apartment door is. Someone opens it to enter the party with a case of beer in their hands, and as soon as they're through, I exit with…what's his name? I don't think I caught it.

It doesn't matter.

We stride across the hall and to Ivy's and my apartment. I open it immediately and tug him inside.

He glances around once. "You live with Ivy?"

"You know Ivy?" I ask.

He shrugs. "Everyone knows Ivy. She and Dustin are a power couple."

"Right…" I say, seizing his hand again and tugging him down the hall to my bedroom. The last thing I want to hear is my brother's name followed by the notion that they're the most adorable couple to be together on the face of this planet. And the last thing I need is to be jealous of it while a hot guy is following me to my room.

We stumble a little along the way, and when I reach my room, I fling the door open and turn to face him again. My hands slide around his trimmed waist, and our lips find each other's again. The kiss is just as desperate as when we were at the party, and we only part for him to fling his shirt off, revealing a set of abs that are so tight they look like speed bumps. His abs give way to a V that disappears into the hem of his pants.

Eager to see what lies beneath, I flick the button of his jeans and he takes the hint, quickly discarding them and kicking them to the side.

I am not disappointed at what I see once his underwear is flung across the room. His cock is beautiful. Can cocks be beautiful? Hell yeah, they can.

Working at the zipper at the side of my dress, I growl in frustration. It's stuck.

"Here," he murmurs. He grabs hold of the dress on either side of the zipper and gives it a tug. The zipper breaks free. He unzips it the rest of the way, and the dress falls from my body and pools around my ankles.

Cold air licks at my stomach, but it's quickly replaced by body warmth as he presses himself against me, reaches around, and unclasps my bra. My breasts spring free and jut against his chest, my nipples pebbled to tight peaks.

He groans as he feels them, cups either side of my face, and kisses me feverishly. Slowly, so as not to make me fall, he backs me up to the bed. The back of my knees hit the edge of the mattress, and we fall together on the soft and plush purple comforter, our lips still locked.

Together, we scoot back on the bed until my head is on the pillow and he's nestled between my legs. His hips rock, and his cock presses against my clit. I groan into his mouth, and he groans back.

Oh god, I can't believe I'm doing this. This is so unlike me. This is beyond the norm for Avery Moore. This—

His hand slides over my shoulder and to my breast where he cups it and then tweaks the nipple. I arch against him, stealing his air straight out of his mouth as I suck in a quick breath.

It's been too long. Far too long.

When I'm a moaning mess beneath him, his hand slides down my body until it reaches my thigh. He hikes my knee over his hip and positions himself. Slowly, he slides inside. I feel every freaking inch and find myself arching into his chest again.

"Fuck," he says into my mouth when he's fully inside me.

His hand by my head curls into the pillow, and his mouth parts against my lips as he inhales sharply. Why is that so sexy? Why does that make me feel so powerful?

He may need time to adjust, but I sure as hell don't. I wiggle my pelvis, and he chuckles against me before moving his hips. The strokes are slow at first like he wants to take his time to savor it. But I really don't give a shit because, immediately, he's hitting a spot that, until now, only I have been able to find.

"Oh my god," I breathe into him. I clench around him, and he curses again.

"Keep doing that and I won't last."

"Can't help it."

It happens again, and his lips part away from mine as he growls. He grabs my other thigh, hikes it around his other hip, and then puts both hands on either side of my head. And then he pulls out and slams into me.

We groan together, and his pace picks up significantly. It's all I can do to hold onto his flexing biceps, feeling that heat coil in my lower abdomen as he quickly strokes my G-spot.

My breathing quickens, and soon - I'm just as surprised as the sex gods - I cum. It explodes out of me, and he rears back, squeezing my hips as he pounds into me.

"Fucking hell," he growls out, his brow pinched in concentration. My hips meet him thrust for thrust as I ride out the waves of pleasure.

Once it subsides, I reach up and tweak my nipples, desperate for another orgasm. I close my eyes in pleasure, and he snaps, "Eyes on me, Sarah."

Sarah? Who's Sarah?

Oh, right. *Me.*

My eyes open and settle on his. I fall into the depths of his hazel eyes that I can see vibrantly even though it's dark in my room. He holds my gaze as I start to spiral again.

I moan again and tweak my nipples harder, and when he says, "God, you're beautiful," I come undone. My pussy squeezes his cock, ripple after ripple, and with several cursed breaths, he pulls out.

Rearing to my elbows, I watch as he pumps himself,

watching even closer as he comes all over my stomach. His shoulders are tense and his head is tipped back as he moans. And when he's finished, his back slumps and he falls back to two hands on either side of my head, his cum cooling on my skin.

As soon as he catches his breath, I almost expect him to leave. That's the normal thing to do, right? On a one-night stand? I wouldn't know. I've never had one.

Instead, he surprises me by kissing me. It's such a soft kiss, and it does something to the weird butterflies in my stomach.

All too soon, he breaks away, getting off the bed, and my heart sinks. The butterflies explode in my stomach as I wait for him to leave without a word. I mean, what did I expect? We met twenty minutes ago. I don't even know this guy's name, even though that was by far the best sex I've ever had.

But I am drunk. He's drunk. We don't know each other. He has every right to leave.

He picks up his shirt and heads back to me. I frown. "What are you doing?"

His brows crease together. "Cleaning you up."

"With your shirt?"

He starts to wipe away his cum. "I didn't see a towel or tissues around."

"Oh." I glance around even though I know he's right and it's too late anyway. Cum is smeared all over his university shirt. "Right."

He flings the shirt back onto his jeans.

"What are you going to wear out of here?"

"I'll figure that out in the morning," he murmurs as he climbs back onto my bed.

"What are…" I blink a few times, confused. "What are you doing?"

He flops down on the bed beside me and buries his

head in the pillow. He's still naked, and I get the perfect view of a perfectly sculpted ass. "Going to sleep."

"Here?"

"Yes, here."

"Um…" Is this okay? The last guy I slept with, like actually slept with in a bed, was *the bastard,* and that was months ago. I've grown used to sleeping alone, but when this mystery guy closes his eyes, I decide I can't deny him. Where would he go? He's too drunk to drive, and he can't return to the party without a shirt.

I flop back onto my pillow, angle my body to grab the comforter from underneath me, and cover myself up. I stare at the ceiling for a moment, watching it spin just a little, before I ask, "What's your name anyway?"

I get no answer, so I tip my head and look at him. His lips are parted, and his face is relaxed. He's asleep. Who the hell falls asleep that fast?

Snorting, I twist to the side, and before I know it, I'm drifting off.

CHAPTER 2
REID RATHE

MY HEAD THROBS. What a fine thing to wake up to. I knew I was doing too many shots last night. I knew, and I was stupid enough to take another.

With my eyes tightly closed against the throb that's easing with every passing second, I let the sound of birds outside wash over me. Surprisingly, with all the shots, I didn't black out. I remember everything. Vividly. And I know exactly where I am, too. My heart stutters as I take in the unique smell that I couldn't get enough of last night. The smell that stuffed itself up my nose and I knew I was a goner.

Her smell.

When I hear the soft breathing of another, I slowly open my eyes. Lying next to me in an unfamiliar bed in an unfamiliar room is...I rack my brain, trying to remember her name. It takes me a moment, but I remember her sweet voice telling me her name was Sarah.

Sarah...

She doesn't look like a *Sarah*. With her soft features, curled and almost-black hair, and a few freckles dotting her nose, the name doesn't portray her beauty. It's too ordinary.

My fuzzy gaze travels lower, sharply focusing when I realize that her shoulders are bare. A comforter is covering her body, but she's definitely naked.

My cock immediately hardens at this realization, and I take her in. Even though she's breathing softly, I remember how she breathed when I was buried inside her. I remember the face she made when she came all over my length, squeezing it tightly. The thought alone makes me bite my knuckles.

Focus on something else, Reid.

A few more freckles dot her shoulder, and my fingers itch to reach out and touch them, but I hold them back. I lift my arm and look down at my body instead, finding myself completely naked and completely uncovered.

Shit. Did I really just plop down on her bed, completely naked, and pass the hell out after sex?

Yes. Yes, I did.

One-night stands aren't typically my thing. I don't do them. It was ingrained in me as a teen not to get someone knocked up from senseless sex by my parents. They didn't tell me why at the time, but I now know it was because of what I'll inherit when they pass their empire down to me, something I'm not and have never been interested in.

That didn't stop me a few times though. I was a little wild as a teen. The few times I have had one-night stands, it was a mess afterward, and I quickly learned my lesson. Since then, I'm not the kind of guy to meet a girl at a party and screw her in the next five minutes of swapping names, no matter how attracted I am to her. No matter how good her lips taste. No matter how her eyes shine with interest for me. Just me. Not for the car I drive. Not for my parents' bank account. Just me.

Briefly, I run a hand over my face and then look back at her. What do I do? Do I wake her? God, I can't do that. She was just as drunk as I was last night, and she probably won't remember a thing that happened. I'm honestly surprised that I do. I remember every detail vividly. How her body fit to mine. How her curves felt under my hands.

Anyway, she will probably freak the hell out and kick me out before I can get my pants on.

My phone dings, and I look over her sleeping form to the floor where my jeans are, my phone tucked into a pocket. I sigh a little and try to peek at the sun through the sliver of opening in the curtains. I know exactly who is texting me, and by the position of the sun, I'm late as hell.

Carefully, I crawl off her bed, working hard not to jostle her. Not to wake her.

When I'm clear of the bed, I pad across the carpet and snatch up my jeans. I slide the phone out of my pocket and read the text. Or, rather, the stream of them.

Dustin Moore
What happened to you last night, man? You disappeared.

Not going to lie, I'm hurt I didn't at least get a goodbye.

I can't help the grin. I know he's joking. He's my best friend; people joke about our bromance all the time.

When we first started college two years ago, we didn't know each other. We met at *one* party, and we hit it off immediately. That was back when I was just getting on my feet without my mother and father's noses breathing down my neck. It was my first bout of freedom, and Dustin took me under his wing and showed me what life was like when I wasn't surrounded by money. He reminds me of the little things that matter more than the things that money can get me. A friend like him doesn't come around often.

I continue reading.

Dustin Moore
I'm at the gym.

Okay, I'm inside and I don't see your wimpy muscles anywhere.

The grin resurfaces. I've been lifting weights since high school. I'm far bigger than him in the muscle department, having introduced him to it a few weeks after we met. He never misses the opportunity to try to make his muscles seem bigger.

Dustin Moore
Seriously. Some girl is staring at me and I need you to turn her away. Where are you?

I glance back at Sarah and then reply to the text.

Reid Rathe
Sorry, got held up. I'll be right there.

Setting the phone on the floor, I quickly slide on my underwear and jeans and then pick up my phone again, slipping it into my back pocket. I pluck up my shoes and my messed-up shirt and quietly exit the room, making sure the knob doesn't latch too loudly.

I stand there for a moment, feeling obligated to at least say goodbye to the woman sleeping on the other side of the door. She deserves more even if I don't really know her.

The sound of a cabinet opening and closing in the kitchen makes me freeze, however. Ivy is here. She's awake, and she's here. And I'm fucked.

Maybe not. Maybe I can get out of this…somehow.

I cringe as I make my way very stealthily down the hallway. If she catches me sneaking out of her roommate's room, I'll never hear the end of it.

Ivy isn't the type to let crap go either. She'd try to play matchmaker, and honestly, as good as that sounds—because I'm dying to get to know the girl I slept with last night—I don't know if Sarah would be into it. I have no idea where she even stands concerning relationships. She could be one of those girls who aren't interested in them until after they have their degree in their hands.

It doesn't matter. Not in this moment because I have to get out of here without Ivy catching me.

When I get to the living room, I peek my head around the corner and into the kitchen. Ivy has her back turned toward me, hands in soapy water, her red hair up in a bun, and her pajamas all wrinkled. No doubt, she spent the night with Dustin last night and made her way back over when Dustin hit the gym.

I keep my eyes on her, making sure she is completely focused on the dishes before I silently make my way to the door. My heart pounds in my chest, and when my fingers curl around the knob, I open it quickly and step out into the building's hallway. When I shut the door, I grimace because it makes a clicking sound.

Grinding my jaw, knowing there's no way she didn't hear the door shut, I move as fast as I can through the hall, down the stairs, and out to my car. Once I get inside my car, I breathe a sigh of relief. She'll know that someone was sleeping with her roommate, but she won't know who. Hell, her roommate probably won't even remember who, and I admit, that thought stings a little.

I stare at the building for a few more moments. She lives with Ivy. I'll see her again, and then I'll introduce myself to her properly and ask her out on a date to get to know each other better. Even if she doesn't remember me, there's a chance she might say yes. God, I hope so because I can't imagine not being part of her life now that I'm a blip in it. She's far too beautiful to pass up, to let go and pretend that nothing happened between us.

Vowing that this is the plan, I start my car and head out of the parking lot, straight for the gym on the other side of campus. Since it's a Saturday, and morning at that, the roads are pretty clear, and I get there quicker than usual.

Parking the car, I grab my gym bag from the back seat, head inside, and go straight to the locker room, not giving an ounce of care that I'm shirtless. It's a gym. People are shirtless all the time.

Once I'm done changing into shorts and a cutoff shirt, I store my stuff in a locker and nearly jog my way out. I spot Dustin right away on the treadmill, so I head to him. As soon as he sees me, however, he lifts his hand and gives me a middle finger.

I chuckle under my breath, hop on the one beside him, and start the machine. The belt moves right away to the speed I set it, and we jog in silence for a few moments before Dustin breaks it.

"Are you not going to tell me what held you up?"

"Jealous that I didn't give you a kiss goodbye last night?" I send a kiss in his direction.

Dustin scoffs. "I got plenty of kisses last night, and I thank God, in this moment, that none of them were from you."

I peek at him before looking forward again. "So you got laid?"

He reaches over and playfully shoves my shoulder.

"Of course I did. But you're still not answering my question, and I'm beginning to think that you're not going to give me the details. What held you up?"

What the hell do I say? That I slept with his girlfriend's roommate?

At that moment, I nearly jump out of my skin as someone slaps my butt, and hard. A familiar voice booms, "What the hell happened to you last night? One minute, we're doing shots, and the next, you were gone," Jacob says.

"Good morning to you too, asshat," I grumble under my breath, rubbing my backside.

Jacob walks around the front of my treadmill and rests his forearms on the dash. His brown brow lifts, and the weight of both of his and Dustin's stares has me cracking under pressure.

Jacob is built more like me than he is like Dustin in the body department, but he has a head of blond messy hair that most women find attractive...well, according to him. According to him, it's the reason he gets laid so much.

Both Dustin and I met Jacob at the gym. One minute, Dustin and I were waiting for our turn on the bench press, and the next, we were talking and getting along with the guy holding us up: Jacob. The rest is history.

Dustin and I aren't as close to Jacob as we are to each other, but he's managed to become a big part of our life anyway.

"I left the party," is all I give them.

"Why?" Jacob asks.

"Did someone piss you off?" Dustin chimes in.

I shake my head, although it's happened before. I don't stick around when someone is bothering me, and a portion of the party tends to follow me anyway. "No, nothing like that."

"Then what?" Jacob presses. "I thought we were

having a good time, and then-" Something clicks in his head and his eyes widen. "You left with a girl, didn't you."

It wasn't a question. It was a complete accusation.

I must take too long to respond because a big grin spreads across his face. "It's about damn time."

"Wait, you got laid too?" Dustin inquires skeptically.

Frowning, I look at him. "Is that so hard to believe?"

"Dude—" Jacob interjects. "You could have anyone you want. You should use your looks more often to have your way with the women. What my friend Dustin here is saying is that he's a little shocked."

I rake a hand down my face, gathering the sweat that's starting to bead there. I forgot to get a towel in my mad dash to get to Dustin. I answer, "It's not what you think."

Dustin slows his treadmill to a walk. "Then, please, explain because you have guilt written all over your face right now."

Dustin knows that I don't sleep around. He knows my past with women. Jacob, on the other hand, only knows a little about it.

"I met someone last night." There. I said it.

Jacob slaps the dash. "And then you banged."

I roll my eyes. "Yes. Okay? Satisfied?"

His grin broadens. "The man, the myth, the legend!"

My eyes widen at how loud his voice got, and I glance around our immediate space to see who heard. The only one around is a girl who has headphones on a few treadmills down. Thankfully, she didn't hear his outburst.

"Jesus, Jacob. Can you say that any louder?" I hiss.

His grin only broadens. "I can if you want me to. Hey, I could even get shirts made for you. I know a crafty girl."

"You mean you've fucked a crafty girl," Dustin interjects.

He shrugs. "To-mate-o, toe-mat-o." He turns his attention back to me. "Was it good? Did you meet her at the party? Which hottie was it?"

I roll my eyes. "Yes, I met her there. We went back to her place."

Dustin scowls at me. "You guys drove? You know how I feel about that."

I wave him off. "She lives in the same building." Over my dead body will I tell him that she's roommates with his girlfriend.

His scowl turns into a frown. "Jessica?" I shake my head. "Dianna?" I shake my head again, and he blows out a breath. "That's literally the only two single women I know in my building."

"Her name is Sarah," I give him.

I can see the wheels turning in his head as he stops his treadmill and wipes his face with a towel that's draped over his shoulder. At least, someone remembered theirs. "I don't know a Sarah."

"Yeah, I get the feeling she was new," I say, becoming out of breath from my short warm-up. I slow it to a walk, knowing that, if I'm going to spot Dustin, who usually goes first, then I have to wrap this up. "I've never seen her at your parties."

Jacob's lips twist to the side as he thinks. "I didn't meet a *Sarah* last night. I wonder how she wandered into the party without knowing us."

I shrug, knowing it was probably Ivy who invited her. "No idea."

"Well, it doesn't matter." Jacob leans his chest into the dash. "Was she a good lay?"

My brows pinch together. I growl defensively, "Is that all that matters to you?"

"Oh shit," Dustin whispers. I glance at him in time for him to add, "You like this girl, don't you?"

I wet my bottom lip as I think it over. There was something about Sarah that caught my attention. Yeah, she's beautiful, but there was something about our brief interaction before the kissing…something that was there. Some sort of connection. There's no way I imagined it. There's no way it was solely because I was drunk.

"Yeah," I answer with a shrug. "I do."

"Holy—" Dustin hops off the belt and mock punches my shoulder. "This is great, man! When do I get to meet her?"

I know he's happy because my last relationship was a shipwreck. I haven't dated anyone since.

Jacob chuffs. "You mean *we*. Because I sure as shit want to see the woman who grabbed his attention."

Internally, I shrug. "I didn't get her number, so I'll probably never see her again."

"Bull crap," Dustin counters. "She lives in my building. You'll see her again."

"You're a stud, dude," Jacob says with conviction. "She'll be back to another one of Dustin's parties for more of your goods."

I roll my eyes, and then I think on it. Shit. What if he's right? What if she comes back to Dustin's party and tries to hook up with me again? I mean, I won't turn her down because, honestly, last night was the best sex I've had in a long time, but I don't want to be used.

As I get off the treadmill and head to the bench press with the guys, my stomach sinks. Because that very well could be the case.

CHAPTER 3
AVERY MOORE

I WOKE up the moment he left the room. He tried to be quiet, but I heard the change of air when the door opened and the subtle whoosh when it closed. Not the latch, though. He was careful with that one.

He was easily the hottest guy I've ever seen, and those eyes...god, those eyes. I remember every detail, every fleck, the pools I got lost in before I brazenly kissed him last night. And I have regrets because I don't even know his name.

Not that it matters. I'll likely never see him again.

I turn over in bed and stare at the spot he was in. The comforter still has a divet in the shape of his body, and faintly, I can still smell him. His lingering scent smells so amazing that I lean over and stick my nose in the comforter for a better whiff and nearly moan when I do.

Groaning, I flop back on my side of the bed. I can not be lusting after a guy. Not so soon. Not after Neil, the bastard, betrayed me. Not after he took my heart and tore it to shreds. Not after he lied. Not after he called me that vial word—the word I knew I was already but it demolished my self-esteem to hear someone I loved say it out loud.

Fat.

But then there's my little one-night stand. I can still feel his hands all over me. He didn't care about my curves. At least, not last night. Not when he was stupid drunk. Not when it was a surefire way that he was going to get laid. Because that's all it was…right?

Of course. He doesn't even know my real name, and I don't know his, and chances are we'll never cross paths again. And I'm okay with that. Getting involved with anyone right now is stupid. I'm just getting my life back together, and throwing myself at another man, albeit an attractive one, is the farthest thing from a good idea.

When my door opens and bangs against the wall, I squeeze my eyes shut and mumble, "Go away."

Ivy's toe pokes my side and I can practically hear the grin in her musical voice when she says, "You had a guy in here last night."

I open my eyes and squint at her. She has a mug of tea between her hands and a grin on her face. She's still in her pajamas though, which tells me she hasn't started her daily routine of Saturday self-care.

When I was living across the country at my old college with Neil, we would talk every Saturday morning on FaceTime. She'd always be in a green face mask and had the phone propped up against the pillows while she painted her toenails a bright red. Always bright red.

"Yes, I did," I admit, trying to bury my face in the pillow out of shame.

"And he snuck out."

I nod into the fluff. Not going to lie, it hurt that he didn't even say goodbye, which tells me one thing: I was a quick fuck. He probably felt ashamed that he slept with someone like me in the first place. Got one look at my curves and bolted.

She sits on the edge of my bed and places a hand on my back as if she knows where my train of thought went.

Even though she and my brother have the most romantic and strong relationship that I've ever seen, she's always understood me. It's like we share the same brain, even when we were miles apart.

Ivy and I met in high school when she started dating my brother. We had run in different crowds. She was the popular cheerleader, and I was the girl eating lunch in the library with my nose in a book. But once she started coming over to my house and hanging out with my twin, we quickly became best friends. My brother jokes about how he has to share her all the time. And now that I'm back, our relationship picked up as if I were never gone for two years. As if I didn't make the biggest mistake of my life moving so far away to be with a boyfriend.

She never judged me for it. And neither did my brother, Dustin.

I had told my brother first about what Neil did to me. I was too ashamed to tell Ivy because she warned me not to go. She never liked Neil, and Neil never liked her. That should have been my first red flag, but I was in love, so I ignored it. And when I told Dustin, he told Ivy, and together, they begged and pleaded for me to come back. To leave that life behind and start over.

Eventually, I gave in and transferred colleges. It was perfect timing, too, because an apartment opened up across from Dustin's, leaving room for me and Ivy to move in together, just as it should have been from the beginning.

She rubs small circles on my back, and even though there's a comforter covering me up, it still soothes the ache that his leaving so abruptly caused. "Men are stupid."

I turn my head and look at her, fresh tears in my eyes. "Are you calling my brother stupid too?"

Her lips twist to the side as she considers it. "Sometimes, yes. But that's why he has me, to make sure he isn't too stupid."

Even though I have tears in my eyes, I still smile a weak smile.

She grins back, moving her hand to my hair, and pushes it from my forehead. "Who was he anyway?"

I turn over, making sure the covers are covering my tits, and look my friend directly in the eye. I could tell her the truth and describe him, but knowing her, she probably knows him. She knows everyone. And then she'd figure it out and march over to his apartment or house or where he lives, and demand that he be a gentleman, come back, and apologize to me for leaving without a word.

No. I can't have that embarrassment. Her knowing he snuck out on me is enough.

"I never caught his name," I say. "The sex just…kind of happened."

She frowns at me. "That's not like you, you know."

"Yeah, I know." Sighing, I glance away from her and stare at my bookshelf across the room. "I guess I was lonely or something. It doesn't matter."

"Of course it matters," she says softly. "Your heart lives in your vagina, sweetie. You pride yourself on not spreading your legs for just anyone."

I laugh without humor. "Yeah, and look where that got me. I've only ever had sex with Neil. God, I should have never given him my virginity."

"Maybe this is a good thing," she says after a pause.

Snapping my gaze back at her, I ask, "How is this a good thing?"

"Well, I mean, how was the sex?"

"Absolutely mind-blowing." Which is a great feat because, when I'm drunk, it's very hard to cum. I can never focus, but he ripped it right out of me, hitting just the right spots and tipping me over the edge.

The sex was completely different than it was with Neil and his Sharpie-thin dick. Worlds apart.

"Exactly."

"I'm still not following."

She grabs my hand and helps me sit up in bed. Then, she stands up and heads to my window, whipping open the curtains and keeping her back to me as I get up and search for clothes in my closet. I pick sweatpants and a graphic T-shirt. "You're getting yourself out there," she explains. "You're testing the waters for what might come. And who knows, maybe you'll see this guy again—sober—and hit it off."

I snort, sliding my shirt over my head. "Doubtful."

She turns around just as I'm sliding my sweatpants on with a scowl on her face. "You have such a low opinion of yourself. It pisses me off. You know what Neil said to you isn't true, right?"

Huffing, I head to the mirror on the wall, snatch a ponytail from a small stand next to it, and put my hair up in a messy bun. "Ivy, I gained fifty pounds while I was with Neil. He wasn't lying. I am fat."

She comes up behind me and rests her chin on my shoulder. In the mirror, she holds my gaze. "I think you're hotter with your curves. You were always so skinny that you looked sickly. The curves suit you."

"You're just saying that because you're my best friend, love me, and are obligated to make me feel better about myself."

The hand that's not holding the mug comes down quickly on my butt. "Have I ever lied to you?"

I yelp and whip around to face her.

She places a hand on her hip and waits for my answer. "Well, have I?"

Thinking it over for a moment, quickly going through memories, I finally shake my head. I can't think of one moment she lied to me. She's always been there for me, through thick and thin, and she's always, *always* told me the truth, even when I didn't want to hear it. Even when I was a love-struck, nerdy teen, too blinded by the fact that someone was looking my way to see that the football player I was dating was an asshole.

"See? I'm telling you the truth. You're a hot chick who has something to grab onto. Don't be ashamed of it."

I hear her words; I feel her truth, but it doesn't sink in.

Instead of glancing at my body in the mirror like I want to, I leave my room and head across the hall to the bathroom where I start brushing my teeth. Ivy follows me, and I get the feeling that she knows I need the company. I do. She isn't wrong.

I study her in the mirror as she moves her tea bag around in the mug and leans against the doorframe.

Unlike me, who started college right away, Ivy took two years off to work. Her parents wouldn't help her pay for college, so she had no choice but to be responsible. Me? I paid for college in other ways. Ways that include a photoshoot that Neil never learned about. It included me in a bikini, posing for a camera issued for a men's "sports" calendar of some kind. At the time, I had a body that was sure as hell not this one, and I flaunted it for the money. I didn't think twice about it, and I had no problems keeping the secret from Neil, but I couldn't keep something like that from Ivy.

Right before I left for college, when the calendar was mailed to me, she found it on my childhood nightstand and stole it for herself so that she could keep it for moments of reminiscing when we're old and senile. I didn't argue with her. We have every intention of raising hell in a nursing home together, and if that includes showing all the old men's love interests of me in a two-piece swimsuit, then let the hellraising begin.

I briefly wonder what she did with it. I even pause in scrubbing my teeth to ask her, but then I think better of it. She probably has it tucked away in a sentimental box somewhere.

"I wonder, if you described him to Dustin if he'd be able to identify him," Ivy says absentmindedly.

I groan as I rinse my mouth and spit. "Just drop it, Ivy."

"Absolutely not. No one ditches my best friend."

Exiting the bathroom, she follows closely behind as I make my way to the kitchen for a glass of water. "I am not going to describe him to my brother."

"Why not?"

I fill up a cup of water and down it as quickly as possible. Wiping my mouth, I set the empty cup down and turn to her. "Because then I'll have to tell him that I got laid. You know how he got about Neil. He hated him as much as you, and he was ready to go across the country to kick his ass when he found out what Neil did to me."

"Exactly." She curtly nods. "You should tell him."

I shake my head. "Definitely not. He'll hunt the guy down."

"He's just being protective."

"I don't need him to protect me. I just need him to be my brother." And nothing could be more true.

Dustin and I weren't always this close. When we were younger, I did something unspeakable to him that caused him to not talk to me for a year straight. Living in the same house, eating at the same table, riding in the same car, and not one single word, no matter how hard I tried to apologize. And then one day, he started talking to me again. Little words here and there that eventually grew into sentences that eventually turned into conversations.

I would do anything - *anything* - to make sure that my brother doesn't pretend that I don't exist again. That year was hell on me. I still carry the shame of what happened that made him shun me to begin with.

She considers me carefully. "I still think you should talk to him about it."

"There's nothing to tell."

"Well, do you want to see this guy again?"

Shrugging, I cross my arms over my chest and lean a hip against the counter. "I don't know. Maybe? I mean, what would it matter? I shouldn't be focusing on men anyway."

"Oh, it matters. You can be all nonchalant about it, but I can tell…you like him."

"I don't know him."

She points at me. "But you want to."

I frown at her for seeing right through me and pointing it out. "What's this have to do with my brother?"

"Well, if you don't want to see him again, you can make sure that he doesn't invite him to any more parties. He would in a heartbeat, you know."

Waving a hand dismissively, I push off the counter, head to the living room, and plop down on the couch. The nail polish is already out on display on the coffee table, and as Ivy follows me, she sits down next to me and picks up her red polish. "I know he would, which is exactly what I don't want him to do."

"Why not?"

"Because I don't want to be the bookworm sister who

tags along with her popular brother. I don't want him going out of his way to make sure I fit into his world."

She props her foot on the edge of the couch and twists the nail polish open. Immediately, its scent fills my nose. "He wants you in his world, you know. He's not doing it because he pities you. He's genuinely happy that you're here, and he just wants to share his life with you."

I look over the nail polish and choose a lavender color. "I know, but I can't stand in his shadow." It's why I didn't tell that guy last night my real name. I pretended to be someone else so that he didn't see me as the twin of the infamous Dustin Moore, someone untouchable. "Let me fit into his world my own way." If that's even possible.

She thinks it over for a moment and then shrugs. "Okay."

I whip my head to her. "Okay? That's it?"

Shrugging again, she starts painting her toenails. "Yeah. I can respect what you said, and I get it. I'll drop the subject. Let's start a new one."

Swiping the brush over my big toenail, I ask, "Are you ready for classes to start Monday?"

Groaning, she answers, "No. I mean, I've had two years off of school, and I'm dreading all the homework again."

I chuckle under my breath. "You get used to it."

"At least, we share a few classes. We can have study nights."

I nod, and we fall into a comfortable silence as we continue to primp our feet. Unlike with other people, where the silence has to be filled, Ivy and I are comfortable with not speaking at all. It's what I love most about her. There are no expectations. I can be exactly who I am, and I couldn't ask for a better person in my life.

Right now, she and Dustin are all I need, and that's enough for me.

CHAPTER 4
REID RATHE

IN THE COURTYARD, with the afternoon sun beating against our backs, I stand in line with Jacob for the best pastrami on campus. No. In the city. Everyone knows it, too, because the line is always ridiculously long. To prove that point, we've been standing here for twenty minutes.

There are two girls in front of us, clearly friends, and Jacob is shamelessly flirting with both of them. One, in particular, keeps staring at me, waiting for me to chime in, waiting for me to flirt back, but I keep my eyes straight ahead, staring at the menu above as if I'm contemplating the side I'm going to choose when I know damn well I'll get the same thing I always get. Sea salt and vinegar chips. Jacob may be interested in them, but I am not.

Two days ago, I met the girl of my dreams. That's what I'm calling her now, and I only know her name. Pathetic, I know.

Not only has she actively been in my dreams, but I find myself searching for her across campus when I'm out and about. Also, I may or may not have been hanging out with Dustin more often at his place, hoping that I might catch a glimpse of her in the apartment building's hallway or out in the parking lot.

No such luck, and I'm growing frustrated.

I scrub the back of my head and blow out a breath as Jacob gets the girls' number, promising to invite them to the next party we throw.

Giggling, they turn back around just in time for them to order their food.

Smiling at me, Jacob pockets his phone. "Dude, that one girl was eye-fucking you."

I stuff my hands into my pockets. "Not interested."

He rolls his eyes. "You're never interested. God, sometimes I wonder if you're gay."

I swivel my eyes to him and pin him with narrowed eyes and he holds up his hands in surrender. "Fine, fine. You're not gay, not that there's anything wrong with that, but I mean…she was hot, and she was into you, man."

Shrugging, I pull out my wallet as the girls pay for their sandwiches, knowing our turn is next. "I hadn't noticed."

Jacob rolls his eyes and pulls out a wadded and wrinkled twenty-dollar bill from his pocket. "I take some mindful happiness knowing that you at least got laid this past weekend."

We step forward and order our sandwiches as the girls disappear with their food. The food court has a few different venues to order from: a taco hut, a burger joint, and a vegetarian stand. It's on the other side of the campus than the cafeteria, a place we tend to avoid if we can help it.

As we wait for our sandwiches, we pay, keeping our conversation nonexistent, but I can see that Jacob has more to say on the matter.

"Just speak," I say with annoyance.

"I think my silence speaks volumes about knowing

how you're hung up on a girl who didn't even give you her phone number."

I squint at him, my irritation now visible on my face. "I passed out right after sex and left the next morning before she woke up. There was no time to get her phone number."

He chuckles and shakes his head.

"What?" I demand.

"Not your finest moment, was it?" he says, poking my shoulder. "Sneaking around so that you don't get caught with your pants down, literally."

Our order is placed before us, and we pick it up and start walking toward an empty table. "Do you have a small dick or something?" he asks as we sit down.

"What? Why would you ask that? Better yet, why would you assume that?"

He shrugs and brings the sandwich up to his mouth. After taking a bite, he says, "Because you barely use it."

I snort and open my bag of chips. The smell of vinegar reaches my nose, making my mouth instantly water. "You know I'm not like that. I don't have senseless sex."

"Except the other night," he points out. His finger jabs in my direction.

"It wasn't senseless," I growl.

He frowns, studying me. "You act like you're in love."

I wave him off after popping a chip in my mouth. "Not in love. I'm not an idiot."

"But you can't get over the girl. God, you're like a chick."

Shaking my head, I mumble, "I don't know why I hang out with you."

He grins around a mouthful of food. "You'd be lost without me. I bring joy to your life. Admit it."

I close my eyes and fight the urge to groan, but he isn't wrong. He has a certain quality about him that makes life a little more fun. Especially at a grueling university and a heavy homework load.

"Come on. Admit it."

Pinching the bridge of my nose, I growl, "Fine. You're fun. Happy?"

Settling into his chair, he takes a huge bite of his sandwich. "Yep."

I open my eyes and drop my hand back down the table with a thump. "You just wait. Someday, you'll be chasing after a girl."

He wrinkles his nose. "Hopefully, I'll have her number if I do."

"You're never going to let that drop, are you?"

He smirks. "Never."

I curse under my breath and look away. Hearing a familiar laugh, I look in the direction of the sound and spot Ivy, Dustin's girl. She's popping a tortilla chip into her mouth. "Ivy's here."

Without swiveling, Jacob asks, "Dustin too?"

I shake my head.

"I'm surprised she's not sitting with us."

Lifting a brow in his direction, I say, "Because you tease her endlessly. You flirt, and not only does it make her uncomfortable; it pisses off Dustin. I wouldn't sit with you either."

He grabs a napkin and swipes the sauce off his upper lip. "Her loss. I'm a catch."

I snort again.

"Where's Dustin anyway?" he asks with a scowl.

"He doesn't get out of economics for another hour."

He stares blankly at me.

"What?"

"It's a little pathetic that you know his schedule."

I shrug. "We compared classes to see if we had any together."

"The bromance is strong with you two."

The corner of my mouth tilts up in a half smile. "Jealous?"

In a mocking tone, he says, "Completely."

Ivy laughs again, and my eyes immediately shoot back to her. As Dustin's best friend, I feel like it's my duty to keep my eye on her just to make sure she isn't getting hit on or something. She's a pretty girl, so it's not impossible, and even though she's dating one of the most popular guys at the college, it doesn't stop some men.

She's leaning toward someone, and I move my gaze to the girl next to her. Only to freeze.

My blood runs hot and cold at the same time. Relief and fear, because there she is. The girl. Sarah. My obsession. She's sitting right next to Ivy, laughing with her over something they shared.

She's just as gorgeous as I remember, if not more so in her casual wear of jeans and a sweater, her hair in a messy bun. There's minimal makeup on her face, a lot less than there was this past weekend, and I find the lack of it makes her even more attractive.

Our time together surfaces in my head, the way her head tilted back as she moaned beneath me, the way her unique scent swirled around my nose, the way her lips fit perfectly to mine.

And then her eyes. I can see them perfectly from here, and I know if I keep staring at them, she'll eventually look my way.

I wonder why she decided to come to this college. I wonder what she's majoring in. I wonder what her favorite color is, favorite smell, favorite food. I want to know all the things about her, and I'm dying to get up from this chair, go over there, and sit next to her to find out. But I know that'd make her uncomfortable, especially in front of Ivy, who probably has no idea that she slept with me. If she had, Ivy would have approached me by now, and since she hasn't, I can only assume that she doesn't know.

"Dude," Jacob says, snapping his fingers in front of my face. "Who are you staring at?"

"No one," I lie, going back to my sandwich. Now that I've found her, I don't want to let her out of my sight, but I also don't want Jacob to know who she is, who I'm staring at, who I'm longing after. I'll just have to find a way to approach her when she's alone if I can find her again. The thought isn't pleasing, but if she stumbled into my path only a few days after meeting her, then it'll happen again.

"You're a terrible liar." He turns in his chair and surveys the people sitting and enjoying their lunch. "Who is it?"

"Drop it, Jacob," I growl under my breath.

Slowly, he turns back to face me, a wide grin on his face. "You found her, didn't you?"

I flex my jaw and stare at my food, forcing myself not to look Sarah's way. "I don't know what you're talking about."

He throws a chip at me, and it hits me in the peck, only to drop to the floor between my legs. "You totally did. Dude, you had hearts in your eyes for a good minute before I said anything. Which one is she?" Desperately, he looks around again before turning back to me. "Come on, who is she?"

"None of your business," I say, flicking my gaze back to his.

"Why do you got to be like that, man? It's not like I'm going to go over there and stick my tongue down her throat, though you probably should. Stake your claim, dude."

I look up at the ceiling and sigh. "I'm going to not do

that. Besides, if I went over there, I'd cause a scene in front of her friend."

He leans forward and whispers, "You have a plan, don't you?"

"Yes. No." I frown. "Yeah, not really."

He shrugs as if what he's going to say next is going to piss me off. "So just continue to stare at her and have her disappear on campus again."

"Unhelpful.". The last person I should be taking advice from is Jacob, but he isn't wrong, which only serves to make me even more angry.

"What are you going to do about that one chick?" he murmurs.

Without having to use her name, I know exactly who he's talking about. I'm supposed to be dating another girl. A girl my parents have set out for me to marry. A girl who goes to this college, just like me. It's complicated, but I try not to think about it. I don't dream of this other girl. I don't fantasize about her.

"Dorothy?" I ask.

"What a name that is," he says, laughing. "What were her parents thinking?"

Shifting uncomfortably in my seat, I answer, "It's a family name I guess."

"You snooty rich people." He pops a chip in his mouth and crunches down. "Of course, they want to carry on a legacy name. Anyway. Does this mean you'll call off this future engagement? Because if you ask me, you're letting your parents dictate who you spend the rest of your life with after you graduate."

I flex my jaw, knowing he's right. It's because of my last relationship that they don't trust me to make wise decisions anymore.

"I was never interested in her to begin with," I admit.

I was just going through the motions after a terrible heartbreak.

"So then, tell your parents no, and go after whoever this hottie is."

"It's not that simple," I grumble under my breath.

"Sure it is. It's a two-letter word."

"You have no idea what it's like to be me, do you?"

He lifts an eyebrow. "Good looks with a lot of money? No."

I tighten my hold on my chip bag. "I don't have a lot of money. I have an allowance to get me through college. It's not like I can tap into the family money whenever I want to." Which is something my last girlfriend found out about and promptly left me after I fell hard for her. I was messed up for weeks, and after that, my parents picked someone out for me who would look good on their future and their empire's future.

"Sure, sure," he says around a chip.

I roll the tension from my neck. "Let's talk about something else."

Considering me carefully, he says, "I don't think I've ever seen you hung up on a girl. Not like that one chick."

Jacob came into the picture at the tail end of my last relationship. He saw the part where I recovered from the heartache. Helped pull me out, actually, and showed me that there was hope for me with his jokes and teasing. That there were other fish in the sea and I'd find my place among the fish.

And I think I have.

I just have to figure out how to go about this. And that's not the only hurdle I have to go through.

"Let me guess; you have some wise-ass joke about it," I say, sneaking a careful glance in Sarah's direction. They're standing and getting ready to leave the courtyard. Panic rises in my throat, knowing that she's going to disappear from my sight again, but I try to calm myself by taking a few deep breaths. I'll find her again. I will. I just have to play my cards right.

Jacob shakes his head. "Nope. None. It was just an observation."

"That's rare," I say, turning my focus back to him once Sarah and Ivy leave the premises and head back into a building, bookbags slung over their shoulder. My heart patters a different pattern, knowing she's no longer in my line of sight.

He frowns as he considers himself. "Yeah. Yeah, it is."

Sighing, I change the subject. "When is your next class?"

Checking his watch, he grumbles under his breath and wads up his trash. He stands, and I stand with him, following him to the trash by the taco hut. "In ten minutes. I gotta get going."

"Yeah, me too," I admit as we throw our trash away.

Before he leaves, Jacob clears his throat. "What are you doing tonight?"

"Going to Dustin's family's house for supper. You?"

He runs a hand through his hair. "Probably heading to the courts and playing some ball. Was going to see if you wanted to come."

Walking backward to the direction I need to go for class, I say, "I'll hit you up when we're done, see if you're still there."

He nods and gives me a wave as he walks off in the opposite direction.

CHAPTER 5
AVERY MOORE

SITTING ON MY BED, I stare at all the textbooks scattered across my comforter. Highlighters, pens, and pencils lie next to my thigh, and my laptop sits to my right. To say I'm overwhelmed is an understatement.

The music playing on my phone in the background does nothing to soothe my nerves, either.

When I transferred here, I thought Smithson University would be an easier college. I don't know why I thought that. Probably because I hadn't heard the rumors that they pile it on. Literally. My backpack couldn't fit all the textbooks, and I was forced to carry several in my arms just to walk home.

Sweat was dripping down my back, despite fall's cooler breeze. I had come in the door, glared at Ivy when she nearly spit out her tea from my frazzled and my out-of-breath state, dropped my books on the bed, and showered.

Now I sit here, in comfortable clothes, staring at what may very well be my death. Death by homework. And the majority of it is due at the beginning of the week. My gosh, this is just one day of classes. I have a whole set of new ones tomorrow and the day after that.

I suppose I should count my blessings that I have a few days to complete them, but with what we'll be getting tomorrow, I'd bet my last dollar that I'll have more.

I sigh and flop back on my pillow, my laptop sliding off my lap and onto the highlighters. I've never been afraid of homework and studying. I was a bookworm in high school and a bookworm in my last two years of college. Unlike my smart brother, I've always had to work hard to get the grades I needed. And because of that and hours of my nose stuck in a book trying to soak up as much as I could, I never gained the social skills to be anything but an introvert.

Neil hated that about me. He was an extrovert through and through. He never understood why I had to try so hard and often held it against me, for reasons I never could fathom. So I had to study to get good grades. That makes me what? A large percentage of the student population?

He never told me, but I get the feeling his grades were horrible and he was projecting his problems onto me.

"Not my problem, anymore," I tell myself as I stare at the ceiling.

Honestly, I should wash my hands of him. But he was a big part of my life, and then what he said to me, and the things that he did to ultimately break us up for good, were a true hit to the ego and self-esteem.

I swivel my head to my right and glance at myself in the mirror. Even lying down, I can see my curves.

Slowly, I lift my shirt and stare. My jaw flexes, and disgust fills me. It's a miracle that I got laid, but it was dark, and he couldn't see anything, and he was probably just as drunk and desperate as I was.

I run my hand over my stomach. I should do something about the weight. If I don't like it, I should do something about it, right?

My phone's alarm goes off, and I slide my shirt back into its proper place. I sit up and turn the alarm off with a simple tap of my finger. With one last glance at my homework, I slide off my bed. It'll have to wait until later. I promised my parents I'd come to dinner tonight, a celebratory meal for having us all together once again.

But we're all different now. Everything is different. It doesn't feel the same, and knowing I'm going to have to put a smile on my face when I feel so dark inside is not something I look forward to.

Heading to my closet, I grasp a dark gray sweater that I'm told by Ivy flatters my curves. It pairs well with my black leggings and falls mid-hip. Next, I throw my wet hair up into a messy bun. My parents don't care what I look like as long as we all get there on time.

My phone chirps, and I head to my bed, pick it up, and read the text.

Dustin
Outside waiting for you.

He's supposed to give me a ride. There's nothing wrong with my car, but he insisted we could carpool. It hadn't been a hardship to agree. I love my brother, and I know the car ride will be filled with a lot of laughter, like usual. And I desperately need a good laugh.

Without a backward glance in the mirror, I head out of my room, down the hall, and into the living room. Normally, Ivy would come with us—she's considered family now for as long as they've been dating—but she had to work at the diner tonight.

I flick off all the lights and my phone chirps again.

Dustin
Still waiting.

I roll my eyes and swing the door open. "I'm coming, I'm—"

I freeze in the doorway. Leaning against the wall next to Dustin's door is…holy mother…it's him. *The* him. The guy.

He's texting on his phone, but even with his eyes downcast, I can still take in his features. He's dressed casually in a pair of dark jeans that hug what can only be thick thighs. The light blue shirt he's wearing forms to his body, showing off more muscles. Was he that muscular the other night? I only distinctly remember his face…and the sex of course. I mean, I knew he had muscles, but this much muscle?

When I say nothing more and continue to stand in the doorway, he lifts his attention away from his phone and settles it on me. A slow smile spreads across his face, almost like the cat got the mouse.

I gulp.

I thought I'd never see him again, but there he stands, hot as ever, his eyes on me, his smile directed at me.

He pockets his phone and crosses his arms.

I mentally curse. What is he doing here?

"Took you long enough, Avery," Dustin grumbles.

His words snap me from my frozen state. "Sorry," I say as I slowly shut the door behind me and step farther out into the hallway. It's the only word I can manage at this moment.

"Avery, huh?" my one-night stander says, the grin still on his face.

Dustin turns to him for a moment and then introduces us. "Avery, this is Reid, my best friend. Reid, this is Avery."

I clear my throat and fidget, remembering that I had told Reid my name was Sarah. Crap. *Crap, crap, crap.*

"She's my sister," he continues.

"The sister you always talk about," Reid murmurs, his eyes still glued to me. "I didn't know she moved in across from you."

Dustin rubs the back of his neck. "Must have slipped my mind."

"Were you at the party the other night?" Reid's grin broadens even wider, and I know, just by that look, that he remembers me.

I glance away, "I might have been."

"She probably left before you got there," Dustin chimes in. "She didn't stay long."

Wetting my bottom lip, I feel heat redden my cheeks. If only he knew.

"That's too bad," Reid murmurs. Sarcastically, he adds, "I definitely would have remembered you."

I flick my gaze back to his, pleading that he doesn't spill our secret. His eyebrows raise at our silent conversation, but he says nothing, thankfully.

Dustin picks up on our silence, on the look on my face and the expression on Reid's. "Am I missing something?"

"No!" I say too quickly. "He just…ah—no. We should get going."

"Yes, we should," Reid says, pushing off the wall.

I frown and my heart picks up pace. "We?"

"He got invited too," Dustin says, flicking his thumb over his shoulder at his best friend.

My stomach drops. This can't be happening. What did I do to deserve such treatment from the universe? I can't ride in the same car with the guy who smells like heaven. "Um. You guys go ahead. I forgot my keys inside. I'll just drive myself."

Dustin scowls. "You will not."

"Dustin-"

"Oh come on, Avery. Don't be stubborn."

Reid tucks his bottom lip into his mouth to hide the smile at my panicked state. Of course he'd find this funny, the guy who, just by appearance, seems to have all of his shit together. Whereas me...I'm a hot mess all year round.

Dustin continues, nodding to the inside of my apartment. "Go get your keys to lock up. I'll wait for you in the car."

Just to get Reid's eyes off of me, I duck inside. On shaky legs, I head to the table where my keys are and take several deep breaths. "This is fine. Everything will be fine. He's not interested. It was one night. That's all. We can pretend that it didn't happen, and everything will be fine."

Grabbing my keys, I bravely head back into the hallway, just to stop again. Dustin is gone, but Reid is leaning against the hallway wall right next to my door. "What are you doing?" I ask nervously.

"Do you always talk to yourself, *Sarah?*" His expression is neutral, but I can tell he's upset that I lied to him.

Butterflies beat against the inside of my stomach. "You weren't supposed to hear that."

"Well, I did."

I close the door and lock it, then rest my forehead against the wood, knowing this conversation needs to happen so that things don't blow up around my brother. "And—um—sorry about the name thing. I was drunk, and it was stupid."

"I've been walking around thinking the girl I can't stop thinking about was named Sarah. Although I think you look more like an Avery, I'm a little whiplashed."

Did he say he can't stop thinking about me? That has to be a lie.

Keeping my forehead against the door, I turn my head toward him to meet his gaze. Gosh, is it intense, smoldering, and I know then and there that he means every word that he said. "You should stop thinking about me, then."

"And why's that?"

I lift my forehead off of the door and turn to face him. "Because I'm not interested."

The grin returns to his face. "Liar."

I scowl at him. "I am not."

He tips his head to my apartment. "Did you forget that I just heard you talking to yourself in there?"

Looking away in shame, I bite my bottom lip and repeat myself. "You weren't supposed to hear that."

He brings two fingers to my chin and tips my head back to face him. The feel of his skin, although very minimal, melts my insides. "But I did, and I'm not mad about it. It lets me know that I'm not the only one affected here."

His gaze moves to my lips, and I know exactly what he's thinking. Even though my insides are screaming at me to let him kiss me, I move his hand off my chin and say quietly, "Not going to happen."

I cannot get involved with another guy, my brother's best friend at that, right now. No matter how hot he is. No matter how he stares at me. No matter his pretty words. He left me, for crying out loud. He didn't say goodbye. I was a quick fuck, and that's probably all he wants right now. That's all guys like him want anyway.

"Why?"

"Because I'm not interested," I whisper, glancing at his lips, wondering just for a moment whether they taste just as good as they did the other night.

He smirks, and god, if it isn't the sexiest thing I've ever seen. "Oh, you're interested."

I flick my gaze back to his with pinched eyebrows. "I'm not going to get involved with someone."

"Why?" he asks again.

"Because I know guys like you. I've dated a guy like you. I'm not interested in a repeat."

That must stun him silent because he says nothing as I lock up the apartment and all but jog down the stairs. I need to get away from him before I do something stupid. Something I'll regret.

No. I can't have Reid. He has heartbreak written all over him, and I have no interest in having my already fragile heart broken all over again. I barely survived what Neil did to me. I won't survive it again, especially since he's my brother's best friend.

CHAPTER 6
REID RATHE

I CAN'T BELIEVE she lied about her name. Ten minutes later, in a silent car with Dustin, it's literally all I can think about. Avery was insistent about driving herself. She refused to get into the car.

When Dustin said we were picking up his sister from across the hall, I figured she was just visiting Ivy. Giddy and excited, I had stayed in the hallway with him instead of going to his car, hoping 'Sarah' would answer so I could get another look, so I could see if she remembered me.

Yep. Wouldn't you know it? She remembered me.

Sarah is his sister. His freaking blood. And she lied.

Why did she lie about her name though? It doesn't make sense unless she was just looking for a hookup and nothing serious. She didn't want me to know who she really was even if she didn't know who I really was. It doesn't add up, but I'm not going to pretend that I understand what's going on in her head.

All I know is that it hurts.

Amazingly, however, it doesn't deter me. I want her now more than ever, and knowing she's Dustin's sibling does nothing to stop those feelings. But I have one problem. She says she's not interested in me. I know that's another lie, but she has to have her reasons for saying it, for being so determined to get away from me.

Maybe the name thing and *this* thing are connected. I'm not sure how, but I have her brother sitting next to me. He's an open book to all things Avery, right?

Hiding my grin, I slowly swivel in my seat to look at the side profile of Dustin.

He catches my look from the corner of his eyes. "What?"

I cross my arms over my chest. "So, your sister..."

He glances over at me with a frown. "What about her?"

Deciding to start out easy, I ask, "What's she majoring in?"

He looks back at the road. "I don't know the technical term. She tells me all the time, but I can never remember it. A surgical nurse of some kind. Or something like that. She has two more years left, like us. Why?"

My shoulders rise and fall dramatically as I shrug and look out the front window. "Just wondering."

"She's minoring in Spanish, just like you."

I whip my head back to face him, and then casually roll my neck, trying to hide the fact that he just dropped a bomb on me. If she's minoring in Spanish, we'll likely share the same classes. Hell, she's going into the medical field just like me, so we may share more than just Spanish.

"Is that so?" I say casually.

He nods. "I'm surprised you guys haven't run into each other yet with you going for anesthesiology. You guys travel through the same buildings."

Blowing out a breath, I hide the hammering of my heart. We may not share the same medical classes, at least none that I know of yet, but we do share the same hallways. I hadn't been searching for her going through some of those hallways, but I definitely will now. Even if she made it clear that she wants nothing to do with me, I don't plan on listening because I know she's lying. She wants me, and I want her, so there's no point in fighting the attraction.

Which brings me to my next question. "Is she dating anyone?" Because that could be the reason she's so uptight and standoffish. It could be a guilty soul. God, I hope not, because if she is, I'll be forced to walk away, and I don't know if I can do that.

He shakes his head. "No, thank freaking God."

I frown. "What's that supposed to mean?"

Adjusting his hands on the steering wheel, he angles his body toward mine. "She just got done with an asshole. It's how I got her to move back home. There was nothing left for her at her old college because her last boyfriend destroyed everything for her. And when she finally did agree to come here, she'd sworn off men until she was done with college."

I rub at my jaw, both relieved and disheartened at this news. "Damn. What happened with this guy?"

He flicks his gaze at me. "Not my story to tell. You'll get to know my sister, and then you can ask her yourself."

My eyebrows rise even though getting to know Avery is exactly what I plan on doing. "Must be pretty bad if she wants nothing to do with even dating."

He chuckles without humor. "Dude, you have no idea. I almost went across the country to kill him."

Tapping my thumb on my jeans, I ask, "Why didn't you tell me any of this?"

With a single shrug, he focuses back on the road. "Again, not my story to tell. I didn't want her past to taint what would happen in her future." He bunches his nose. "Don't tell her I'm telling you this."

"You're not really telling me anything," I point out.

He scowls as he comes to a stop at a red light then flicks his gaze to the rearview mirror where Avery follows close behind in her car. "Why are you so interested in this? You could just ask her yourself. She's going to be hanging out a lot with us."

I quickly turn my attention out the window. "No reason."

He is silent for a few moments, and then his voice rumbles, "Absolutely not."

"Huh?" I say, even though I know exactly what's coming next. Dustin's too smart for his own good. I should have known he'd make the connection.

"You're not going to date my sister." His voice is so firm that my stomach sinks.

Slowly, I turn back to face him. His face is set, and he spares me several glances as we hop onto the highway. "Who said I wanted to date her?"

"You're completely interested. You never ask about stuff like this."

I try to shrug indifferently, but I know I've failed when my voice cracks, "Just trying to get to know her."

"Yeah, right. You're getting the scope of things. You're totally interested, and I'm telling you absolutely not."

I flex my jaw, and anger starts to curl and lick at my gut. "Why the fuck not?"

"Dude, I just told you about her bad breakup. And I don't want my friend and family life to mix. If things get messy, I'll have to choose." He shakes his head. "No. No dating my sister. Don't even try it."

Continuing to flex my jaw, I stare out the front window. Now what the hell am I going to do? He's my best friend. And she's the girl I can't stop thinking about.

Can I ignore Dustin? Can I pursue Avery without him knowing and hope that he eventually comes around to the idea? Or do I walk away from Avery completely and try to stuff my attraction to her down so deep that I become someone I no longer recognize? God, that sounds horrible. Why would I do that to myself?

No, I won't do that. Not when Avery and I could maybe—possibly—be the best thing that's ever happened to both of us. Just because I'm selective about the women in my life doesn't mean I'm not a romantic.

Option one it is. I'll pursue Avery without Dustin knowing, and when the time is right, if Avery and I actually become something, I'll tell him.

Sure, he'll be mad for a little while, but he'll get over it.

CHAPTER 7
AVERY MOORE

THE SMELL from the grill is amazing. It fills the entire backyard of my childhood home with a barbeque aroma that makes my stomach grumble with anticipation. My dad is making his famous BBQ ribs, a bit messy to eat but always worth it to scrape the sauce off your cheeks and lick them from your fingers.

He won an award for the BBQ sauce at our county fair when I was ten and has never let us forget about it. Every time he whips out the recipe, he reminds us of that fated day. And every time he reminds us, we all groan even though we're as proud today as we were the day he got that trophy he displays above the fireplace mantel.

In lawn chairs, I sit next to my mom, a glass of tea in each of our hands as we watch the guys play football in the yard. My neighbors are over, a wonderful gay couple that we've grown close to over the years, making the football party five grown-ass men fighting over a ball.

My eyes can't help but track Reid's every freaking move. The grin hasn't left his face since he got here, and what shocked me most is that my parents treated him like he was their own child. My father slapped his back, and my mother gave him a bigger hug than she gave me. She even pecked his cheeks, leaving a red mark from her lipstick. I stood there, dumbfounded.

How often did he come home with Dustin while I was away for two years? Even more so, why had my parents never mentioned his name when I would make my regular Sunday calls to catch up?

My mother reaches over and pats my hand that's resting on the lawn chair's armrest. She looks just like me, except for the graying blonde hair. I get my dark hair and bigger figure from my father. "Have I mentioned how happy I am that you're back?"

I don't tear my eyes away from whatever weird football game they're playing as I answer her, "Only a million times."

"Well, a million and one then. It's been so dull here without my baby girl."

Glancing over at her, I chuckle under my breath. "I'm not that thrilling."

She scowls. "Sure you are. Dustin doesn't like to go shopping or have girl chats. I tried."

I laugh even harder and turn back to the football game. My laughter draws the attention of Reid, and he looks my way, staring a bit too long, and he ends up getting bumped into by my dad. "I wish I was there to see it when you tried."

Like always, her smile is so graceful. I bring the tea up to my lips as she explains, "He didn't come home for a full two weeks after I gossiped about my girlfriends and their sex lives."

Tea flies out of my mouth and onto the dead grass below our chairs. "You told him about their sex lives."

She shrugs. "I had no one else to talk to."

"You could have called," I say, smiling wide and

wiping my chin with the back of my hand. "I would have listened."

Turning to the game, she takes a beat before she says anything. And when she finally does, it's soft. "I didn't want to be a bother."

I frown. "You're never a bother. Why would you say that?"

"Well," she begins, blowing out a breath. "I could tell Neil didn't like you calling home so often. I didn't want to add to…whatever his problem was."

My frown deepens. "That's not true."

She looks at me sidelong, long enough to get her point across. "Every Sunday, you'd get off the phone when he asked you to, and it was never a long conversation. I know it was because he didn't like it when you called home. He was controlling, Avery."

The football game seems to be over because the guys, laughing, head to the grill. I turn to my mother, but I watch Reid. His shirt clings to his body, showing off his muscles with every stride that he takes. "He was?"

She nods. "Very. It concerned me that you always gave in to him."

I look back to her when Reid catches me staring. I didn't miss his grin, however, having been caught red-handed. "Why didn't you say anything?"

She shrugs and tucks a lock of hair behind her ear. "You seemed happy."

"You really thought I was happy?"

Another shrug is my only answer.

Back then, I thought I was. But when I moved out and had some reflection on the travel back home, I realized I was never happy with Neil. He wasn't the same guy I started dating in high school. He had changed, and it wasn't until he had destroyed me that I realized how much. He turned into someone I didn't recognize and, in turn, changed me, molding me to fit to his needs and not my own. It was never a give-and-take. It was always a take.

"Did you ever like him?" I ask, unsure if I want the answer. My mother usually tells it to me straight, so if she's been harboring her dislike for him all these years, I'll be shocked and a little hurt. I've always been a momma's girl, always looking to please her even though that isn't really hard. She's a loving and caring mother, always has been. But to know that I disappointed her by staying with Neil…

She glances away, and I get my answer.

"Why didn't you say anything?" I ask quietly.

She returns her gaze to me and repeats herself. "You seemed happy. I didn't want to be the reason you were heartbroken. Though, I should have said something; I realize that now. I could have saved you the heartache."

"It's not your fault."

She pinches her lips together and then says, "It feels like it, in a way."

I reach over and grip her hand, giving it a squeeze. "I'm doing okay now, Mom." *Sort of.*

Nodding slowly, she squares her shoulders. "Now we just have to get you back on that horse."

I groan and slump in my chair, draining my tea. "I don't know about that."

Reaching over, she squeezes my forearm. "Is there any interest in your life?"

Without meaning to, I flick my gaze to Reid, and being the smart woman that she is, she follows my gaze. A giant smile spreads on her face when she turns back to me. "Oh, my goodness. You like him?"

The frown returns to my face. "I do not."

She chuckles under her breath and leans in conspiratorially, but my attention is still on Reid. I can't help it;

he's a magnet for my attention even if I say otherwise. There's something about him that I just can't wrap my head around, and that scares me. The last time that happened, I dated the asshole who turned me into the relationship shrew that I am today.

He's talking to my brother and one of my neighbors as they hover around the grill while my dad bastes the meat. God, he's gorgeous. Dustin says something to him, and he throws his head back and laughs, and when he brings his head back down, his gaze lands on mine. And...I can't look away. We hold each other's eyes for a good few seconds until one of his eyebrows rises and a smirk takes over one side of his lips.

I shake my head and look back at my mother, who is grinning like a fool, having caught the entire interaction. "You do," she says. She gives my arm another squeeze before returning her hand to hold her drink.

"I don't want to start anything."

She scoffs. "And why not? He's a handsome man, and we've spent a lot of time with him. He'd be perfect for you."

"Yeah, I thought the same thing about Neil, remember?" I swirl the ice in my cup to keep my attention anywhere but on Reid, who is still watching me.

"You were young. Young love is hard to determine who is worth your time and who isn't."

"I'm still young, mom."

She holds up a finger. "But wiser. I trust that you know what's good for you, and *he* is good for you."

"I'm just not ready," I say with a sigh, wanting the subject to drop before we get to the part where it's about my self-esteem.

"But-"

I stand abruptly from the chair. "I'm going to get some more tea."

Without another word, I head to the house and climb the porch steps. I can feel Reid staring at my back the entire way, and it makes my shoulders bunch to have that much attention on me.

Once inside, I head to the fridge and grab the tea pitcher. Quietly, my mind reeling and my eyes on the verge of tears, I fill my cup. Then, I turn around to rest against the counter but startle, finding someone else in the kitchen with me.

The kitchen and the dining room are one space, and Reid is leaning against a dining room chair about ten feet from me. His arms are folded across his chest, and his face is expressionless.

I place a hand over my racing heart. "You scared the crap out of me. I didn't even hear you come in."

"I wasn't trying to be sneaky," he rumbles. God, his voice is like silk. Goosebumps rise over my skin.

We stand there in silence for a few minutes, both of us staring at one another, willing the other to speak what's on their mind. I start the squirm, but instead of giving in, I grab the pitcher and hold it up. "Thirsty?"

He nods. "But not for a drink."

I gulp and grip the pitcher tighter. "What do you want, Reid?"

"You," is his simple answer.

"You don't even know me," I say, shaking my head and putting the pitcher and my glass down. I rub at the goose bumps along my arms. "You can't want someone you don't know."

He raises those beautiful eyebrows again. "Are you telling me you don't feel this weird thing between us?"

I look down at my sandals, a denial on my lips, but I can't bring myself to say it out loud.

"That's what I thought." He takes a step closer. "Why did you lie to me, Avery?"

I snap my gaze back up to his. "About my name?" He nods, and I blow out a breath. "I told you. I have my reasons."

"And I want to hear them."

I jut out my chin, hoping to stand my ground as he steps another step in my direction. "No." I owe him nothing. I won't give in to this feeling between us.

He cocks his head to the side. "What guys have you dated like me?"

Swallowing thickly, I contemplate the way I want to answer him. I should have never told him that. I should have never shared a piece of me with him, a virtual stranger who is trying to shove himself into my life everywhere I turn. "My last boyfriend. You remind me of him."

His jaw flexes, and briefly, I wonder what he knows about my relationship with Neil. Clearly, he knows something because the mention of him has the muscles along the side of his face working. "I'm not him."

I shrug. "You don't even know him. You have no idea if you're like him."

He steps closer, and this time, there's little less than a foot between us. I have to look up to peer into his eyes, but I hold my ground.

Or I try to anyway. I can feel the beginnings of a tremble.

God, those eyes. They beg me to overshare, to spill all of my secrets to see if he can weld the broken pieces of my heart that refuse to mend back together.

I clench my jaw. *I won't give in. I won't give in. I won't.*

"Why won't you give me a chance to prove it to you then?"

"Because I don't know you," I whisper.

"You could know me. I'm a good guy."

I blow out a shaky breath. His nearness is making my

heart skip beats. "Good guys don't have one-night stands."

A small smile plays at his lips. "What about good girls? Because if I remember right, you made the first move."

"I did not," I say, tasting the lie. I look away as my cheeks heat.

Slowly, carefully, as if not to scare me off, he curls his hand under my chin and turns my face back to his. His touch sends a shiver down my spine. "You did," he murmurs.

My breathing picks up pace as his gaze bores into mine. His hand remains where it is, making sure I don't look away from him. A silent communication passes between us once more, and something builds in the small space between us. An electric charge. A tug of war, begging our chests to close the space.

His tongue darts out to wet his lips, and my eyes zoom to it. With his lips still parted, he blows out a shaky breath, and it fans my face, smelling just as delicious as he does.

I shouldn't be feeling something. My heart shouldn't beat harder when another guy is around. I swore off men. I turned my back on them. So why is my body betraying me? Why is my heart begging me to give him what he wants even if I don't fully know what he wants from me?

With that question in mind, I flick my gaze back to his. "What do you want from me?" I ask him quietly.

His eyes are on my lips, but he bends down, and his lips touch my ear when he whispers, "I want you, Avery Moore. More than anything, I want to get to know you. I want you to get to know me. I want to see where this leads because I know for damn sure that I'm not the only one who feels something. It wasn't a one-night stand. It was the beginning of something else, and you and I both know it."

I open my mouth to say something, but his lips press against my jaw, a subtle kiss that makes my heart pound against my ribs. The hand holding my chin moves along the other side of my jaw and to the back of my head, tangling in my hair as he presses another kiss to my jaw, closer to my lips.

The heat of his body presses into mine as he scoots closer. His lips find the corner of my mouth, and it takes everything in me not to turn my head slightly and take his lips with my own. I want to. I've never wanted anything more. What could it hurt? To taste him one more time? To see if there are any sparks?

I bet there would be sparks. I bet it would be mind-blowing.

His eyes look into mine, a question in them, and when I don't reject him, he moves his lips over mine.

The back door slams shut, and laughter fills the house. We separate so fast that my head spins at the sudden absence of him. With a good five feet between us, Reid rubs at his jaw as everyone piles into the kitchen with the ribs on a tray in my father's hands.

What the hell just happened?

A football game plays on the living room television, but the only one watching it is Dustin. The food has been devoured, and our neighbors have returned home. My father is outside, closing down the grill, and Reid is in the kitchen with my mother, helping her wash dishes. I watch them for a moment, but I need space to breathe, our almost kiss still fresh on my mind.

So I step out to the living room with so many questions on my mind that I just need a moment to myself. I forgot Dustin was in here, but it isn't a hardship. Maybe I can learn a thing or two while I have him to myself.

I plop down onto the couch next to him, pretending to be interested in the sport for a few moments before I slouch back and lean my head on his shoulder.

He pats my head absentmindedly and then hoots and hollers when there's a touchdown.

Once he settles down, I start in on the questions. "So, Reid. How did you meet?"

Without looking at me, he says, "At a party."

I chuckle under my breath. "Naturally. Love at first sight?"

He returns the chuckle. "Something like that."

"Does he always come to our house for supper, or do you go to his?"

I don't miss the way his nose wrinkles when he says, "Definitely here."

My eyebrow curves up into my forehead. "You don't like his parents?"

Turning down the volume on the game, he turns to face me, giving me his full attention because, clearly, I'm not going away any time soon. "They're snobby, so no."

I frown. "So you've met them?"

He laughs, but there's no humor. "Oh, I've met them. In their mansion, surrounded by expensive cars."

"So he's rich."

"Who?"

"Reid."

His brows pinch together. "Well, yeah, I suppose. Sort of. I mean, his parents' money is their own. The only money he gets from them is a weekly allowance."

I roll my eyes. Of course he's rich. And he's probably used to getting what he wants because he *is* rich. "I bet it's more than what the average American makes in a year."

"Hey, don't be like that." He taps my nose with his pointer finger. "It's not what you think. He's a good guy, Avery. Nothing like his parents. Don't judge a book before you've read the words."

"So you're telling me that what? They give him money for food and gas, and that's it?"

He shakes his head. "I mean, they do, but they pay for his apartment too."

"And school?" I don't know why I'm acting so bitter. Maybe it's because I had to wear a bikini to pay for mine, and Ivy had to take two years off of school just to pay for hers.

"Avery..."

"What?"

He leans in. "He got into college because he earned it. A full ride because he put in the work."

I glance away, shame gripping me. Well, don't I feel like an asshole now? "So his parents..."

"Yeah, they're a whole other situation." He blows out a breath. "Do you know they want him to marry wealthy? You should have seen them with his last girlfriend. They're totally controlling now."

My heart sinks, though it shouldn't because I'm not interested in him...right? "Oh yeah?"

He turns back to the game and settles back into the couch. "He's not some posh dude like his parents want him to be, and he's not some wealthy ass like you're making him out to be."

"I'm not—"

He glances over at me. "You are. Get to know him, Avery. He's a cool guy once you get past his fancy car and an apartment all to himself."

I bite my bottom lip. "Yeah. We'll see."

Once I fall silent, he turns the volume back up, leaving me to my own thoughts. I mean, if Dustin hadn't told me he was wealthy, I would have never guessed. He doesn't flaunt his money. He doesn't seem like a guy who would, either.

As if he'd overheard us, or fate just has a funny way of sticking him into my life when I'm thinking about him, Reid comes into the living room, his hands in his pockets. "You about ready, Dustin?"

He may be speaking to Dustin, but his eyes are on my face. I squirm a bit in my seat but pretend to be watching the game. I'm not ready to confront the feeling I get when surrounded by all things Reid.

Sighing, Dustin turns off the TV. "Just when it was getting good, too."

"You're leaving?" I ask when my brother stands. I had expected him to ask for five more minutes.

Dustin bends down and gives me a hug. "Jacob wants to shoot some hoops before dark. Want to come? Ivy is meeting us there."

Purposefully keeping my gaze off Reid, I shake my head. I don't think my nerves can take another minute of being in Reid's space. I feel raw around him, exposed, and while that shouldn't be a bad thing, I can't trust him. I don't know if I ever will be able to.

"You two go ahead. I have homework to do."

Dustin pecks me on the cheek and thankfully doesn't fight me on it. Without another word, they both leave, and I blow out a big breath before saying goodbye to my mom and dad and heading back to my apartment.

CHAPTER 8
REID RATHE

IT WOULD BE an absolute miracle if I could get Jacob to stop talking about his fling from over the weekend. He's animated about it, nearly dropping his backpack every few seconds, and he's been going on and on since lunch. Even though I know he's completely oblivious, it's just salt to an open wound.

Why? Because I haven't been able to stop thinking about her. Surprise, surprise. It's not even about the sex at this point. I would take a single glance in my direction to hold me over for another day, just to do it all over again the following day so I can fucking breathe.

As we walk down the hall, I roughly mess with my hair as Jacob prattles on. Why am I so obsessed with this girl? Why can't I get her out of my head?

Even when I look at other girls, knowing that my chances with Avery are probably slim, I just…feel nothing. Sure, I recognize beauty, but Avery has it all, and I know this while barely knowing her. I just know what Dustin has shared with me over the past two years, and I admit, I don't remember much of those conversations.

We almost kissed. Almost. We were so close, and hell,

she was going to let me. I know she wants me as much as I want her. I know we share something that neither of us can explain. I just wish I didn't remind her of her ex, and I don't know if I can overcome that, but I sure am going to freaking try.

She's worth it.

I know she's worth it.

"Are you even listening?" Jacob asks as we head down the wide hallway.

I glance over at him and adjust the strap of my backpack. "Yes," I lie.

"Bullshit," he hisses. "What's her name then?"

A frown takes over my face as I try to think of the name of this girl that he dropped early on in the conversation. I can't think of it, so instead, I say, "I'm surprised *you* even know her name."

He chuckles under his breath as we head to Spanish down this long hallway, squeezing ourselves in between the people in the crowd moving in the opposite direction. "She's memorable, man."

"Sure, sure. What's so memorable? And don't say her pussy, or I'll backhand you."

He holds up his hands, palms out. "That's just one of many things."

I shake my head. "You have no shame."

His grin is wide. "None. I was born without it."

"Clearly," I mutter. "So are you going to have a relationship with this one?"

"What?" His scowl is instant, and I know exactly what his answer will be. "No. Why would you think that?"

"Because you won't shut up about her."

His scowl only deepens, and I laugh. "Admit it. You're smitten."

"Who the hell says smitten these days?" he mocks.

"Me, apparently," I grumble under my breath. I'm aware that he diverted my question, but I'll let him deny it for now. Who knows, maybe he'll be sick of her by the end of the week. If not, then I have plans to get on his nerves about settling down. I know it'll drive him nuts, and it will be totally worth it since he's been driving me nuts on a regular basis.

When we reach the door, he groans. "Why did you force me to take this class?"

I huff. "Because it's good for you. The country isn't just made up of the English language anymore. If you want a good job straight out of college, it looks good on your resume that you'll know more than your native tongue."

Jacob stops, his hand hovering over the handle of the Spanish room's door. I meet his eyes only to find the scowl back on his face. "You're like a mother hen."

I shove his shoulder. "Someone has to keep you in line, or you'd fuck your way to the top and graduate with ten STDs."

His nose wrinkles as he yanks the door open. "That was a low blow."

This level of Spanish is held in a lecture hall this year. Something about not having enough space and giving its old space to a different department. I'm not sure of the details, but I'm sure it pissed off someone that Spanish wasn't important enough to have an actual classroom. Either way, it doesn't bother me. I prefer the lecture hall seats over the hard metal ones of Smithson University's classrooms anyway.

Rows and rows of padded seating with small desks unfolded from the right arm of the chairs travel down until there's an empty space for the lecture podium. Behind that are some rolled-in whiteboards, all currently blank and ready for use. The professor is nowhere in sight, but we're a little early, so that's no surprise.

"Dude," Jacob says, drawing my attention with the point of his finger. "Ivy's here."

Without a word, he makes his way down the middle row, and I follow, my eyes finally landing on Ivy and... *Avery*.

I suck in a deep breath. She's here. Shit, she's here, and for the first time in days, a weight is lifted off my chest.

Today, she's wearing a light gray university sweater with light blue skinny jeans. If she's wearing makeup, I don't see a trace of it. She bends down to get something out of her backpack by her feet, and her loose hair spills over her cheek, but she has yet to notice us.

A smile grows on my face, knowing that I couldn't have planned this better.

I stop Jacob before he can scoot into the seats and make my way in first. Avery doesn't look up from her now-open laptop until I plop down in the seat next to her. She jumps in her seat, and her hand flies to her heart.

"Spanish, huh?" I ask, my voice hushed as both Jacob and Ivy share a look with each other. I'm sure it looks odd that I insisted on sitting next to Avery. I really don't care right now. I couldn't pass up this opportunity.

Nervously, she tucks a lock of hair behind her ear. By doing that little gesture, the smell of her fruity shampoo reaches my nose, and I fight the urge to lean over and take a deeper breath.

"W-What are you doing here?" There's a tremble in her voice that's adorable.

I grin a little when she finally meets my gaze and holds it for longer than a second. "You're not the only one minoring in a second language, you know."

"Oh," she whispers and then clears her throat. "Right."

"Is that a problem?" I ask when she says nothing more and fires up her laptop. Her foot jiggles though, telling me she now has anxiety over me being here.

Frowning, she cuts me a glance. "No," she whispers. "But...can't you sit somewhere else?"

Humor dances in my tone when I say, "No. The other seats are taken."

She surveys the room, the frown deepening. "There are literally fifty other chairs to choose from."

I shrug and pull my laptop out of my bag, making it clear that I don't plan on moving. She's not getting rid of me that easily. "None next to you."

Hissing through her teeth, she says, "What is your *deal* with me?"

Ivy and Jacob lean further forward in their seats, but it's Ivy who asks, "Do you two know each other or something?"

Without looking away from each other, we both lie, "No."

Ivy raises an eyebrow. "Are you sure because-"

"No," we both say again as the professor strides into the room with his papers and packets and a large book balanced in his arms. He sets them down on a table to the right of the podium, and Avery finally breaks eye contact with me, facing forward and squaring her shoulders in determination.

I hide my smirk well, and as the professor starts to talk about himself, his accomplishments, and the expectations of this class, I open up a Word document and start typing a message.

Me
My deal? We almost kissed, and I can't stop thinking about what would have happened if we did.

I turn my laptop slightly toward Avery, and when she pretends not to notice, I clear my throat.

Rolling her eyes, she glances at my screen. A blush creeps into her cheeks before she's completely finished reading, and right this moment, I would give anything to touch them. But she goes back to listening to the professor—not the response I wanted, so I nudge her foot with my shoe. When she flicks her gaze in my direction, I tip my head to the screen.

Sighing again, she opens a Word doc on her computer and types out a response.

I lean over to read it at the same time that Jacob starts to catch on. He leans over with me, but I shoulder him back.

Her
I haven't thought about it at all.

I huff.

Liar.

Her
Am not.

Me
The corner of your mouth twitches when you lie. Did you know that?

She turns a frown at me but goes back to her keyboard.

Her
So what if I have thought about it? It means nothing. Who wouldn't think about some tall guy invading their space and demanding a kiss?

My snort draws Ivy's attention.

Me
You and I both know you wanted me to kiss you as much as I wanted to kiss you.

She shakes her head but doesn't type out anything.

Me
Do you want me to kiss you now, Avery?

It takes her a moment, but she eventually gives in and looks sideways at my screen. In my ear, Jacob whispers with a laugh, "Dustin is so going to kill you. Oh shit, is she the girl from the other night?"

"Keep this to yourself," I growl in warning, keeping my attention on Avery as she types out a response.

Her
I would blow my rape whistle if you tried.

I cannot help the smile that crosses my face. *You wouldn't dare.*

Her
Try me.

Me
Do you even have a rape whistle?

Avery sits back in her seat with a snarl on her lips. That would be a no, then.

I chuckle quietly.

Me
Didn't think so.

She doesn't respond and, instead, crosses her arms over her chest as she pretends to listen to the professor. I look past her and at Ivy, who is glaring daggers in my direction. I wince, knowing she had to have read that conversation just as well as Jacob had.

It tells me one thing though: Avery didn't tell her about us. I'm sure she knows something is up now, so I pull out my phone and send a quick text to her.

Me
Remember how you owe me for saving you from the drunk frat boy at the diner?

She keeps her glare on me as she pulls her phone out of her backpack and reads the screen. Her jaw flexes, but her fingers fly across the screen.

Let me guess. You want me to zip my lips because you don't want Dustin to know that you're practically humping his sister.

Me
Maybe.

She shakes her head.

I don't see the problem here. Did he warn you away from her or something?

Me
He might have.

The look she gives me could kill.

You want me to lie to my boyfriend?

I cringe.

Well, not a lie per se. Just...not say a word. It's not a lie if no words are spoken.

Her
And if Avery wants you to leave her alone?

Me
She doesn't.

Her
Sure didn't look that way.

Me
Look, I know her last boyfriend did a number on her, and I don't plan to do anything to damage her further. I just want to get to know her. I have to get to know her, Ivy.

Ivy reads the text a few times, nibbling on her bottom lip, until finally, she replies.

Okay. But if this goes south, I was not involved in any way.

I flash a grin her way.

Thank you. I owe you one.

Her
Yeah you do.

Satisfied that she won't go screaming to Dustin that I blatantly ignored him about staying away from his sister, I pocket my phone and turn to the professor, trying like hell to tune in to his lesson but failing miserably.

I'm distinctly aware of every move Avery makes. She's stiff as a board, but every now and then, she reaches up and moves the hair from her face. When she types notes out onto her laptop, it stirs the air around us, and a soft scent reaches my nose.

How the hell am I going to get this girl on my side? How am I going to get her to let me in? Because, clearly, that's going to be a huge problem. I'm not backing down, though. No freaking way.

I try like hell to concentrate, but it doesn't happen, and when class is finally dismissed, I don't even realize it until Avery, Jacob, and Ivy are packing their bags.

Since we are sitting near the front, the four of us are the last to leave. Even the professor is gone, having disappeared quicker than the students. As we reach the back row, I give Avery's elbow a tug.

Whipping around, she glares at me. "What?"

Oh no, she's not going to steer me away by having an attitude. "I want to talk to you for a minute."

She blows out a breath, a protest on her lips, but Ivy says, "I'll wait for you outside." She doesn't wait for Avery to reply before she's taking Jacob by the arm and dragging him out of the room.

Once they're gone, I turn Avery to fully face me. Her eyes are glued on my chest, and I take a step closer to her, but she steps back. I take another, and so does she. One more and her back hits the wall by the door. Only then does she meet my gaze, hair falling in her face.

I swipe the hair from her face with a gentle touch, and her eyelids flutter as my fingertips graze her cheekbone. "See? That right there."

Her brows pinch together. "What?"

I run my fingertip along her jaw. "That. The way you react to my touch. I know you feel something, Avery."

She chuffs and glances away. "It's a normal reaction when someone attractive touches me."

My chuckle is deep. It's more than that, but I'll let it slide. "So you think I'm attractive?"

Still looking away, she shrugs. "I'm not going to lie about it. You're hot. End of story."

Something clicks then, and I guide her face back to mine. "Do you think I'm out of your league, Avery?" The way she swallows tells me I've hit the nail on the head. I lean in closer to her and brush my nose against hers. She doesn't fight me on it, so I do it again. "Do you really not see what I see?"

"There's nothing to see," she whispers.

"Oh, you have no idea, beautiful girl." I'm so close that I could kiss her if I wanted to, but I know she isn't in the right headspace for it. We share breath as I admit, "Your brother said you were off limits."

Her chest presses into mine as her breathing picks up. My nearness is affecting her like it's affecting me. "And yet, here you are."

"Because I'm interested, Avery. More than interested."

Her lips twitch, and I know whatever she says next is a lie. "That makes one of us." I curve an eyebrow, letting her know that I know it wasn't the truth. She wets her bottom lip and stutters, "D-Doesn't matter if I am; Dustin said no."

I lift my hand, cup her neck, and run my thumb along her jumping pulse. "You're scared."

She blows out a chuckling breath, but there's absolutely no humor in it. "Well, yeah."

I get the feeling that it's not her brother she's scared of because he loves her to death, so I tell her again, "I'm not your ex, Avery."

She shakes her head, and tears start to prick her eyes. "I need to go."

I search her expression, take in how scared she actually is and how far I can push, and when I decide that she's at her limit, I drop my hand and step away. It's difficult, but she needs to know I'm not going to take what she doesn't want to give. She's too scared right now to give anything. Whatever that bastard did to her, it really messed her up.

She wipes a tear from her cheek and heads to the door. When she's gone, I scrub the back of my neck. Lucky for me, I have all the patience in the world.

CHAPTER 9
AVERY MOORE

I EXIT the Spanish hall in a flurry of emotion. A tidal wave. A great tsunami. Tears prick my eyes, and a sob racks my ribs.

What the hell just happened?

I know exactly what happened. He cornered me again, confronted me, and I just about gave in. What is wrong with me? Why can't I control myself when I'm around him? And how does he get past my defenses with barely a touch?

That's one thing he and Neil don't have in common. Reid could bring me to my knees by just rubbing his hand across my cheek. Hell, he almost did by brushing his nose along mine. With Neil, it was never like that. Sure, I was completely enamored, but not like this. His touch didn't set me on fire. It didn't make me forget my purpose, my conviction.

Ivy is leaning against the wall in the hallway, scrolling on her phone. She doesn't spot me until I'm almost past her, but I catch the surprise on her face as I wipe away a tear and charge forward.

"Hey!" Ivy says, trying to catch up with me. "Hey, slow down!"

Her hand clasps around my upper arm, and she tugs me to a slower pace. Once I don't act like I'm going to continue to charge off without her, she falls into step beside me. "What's wrong?"

I shake my head and take a deep breath. "Nothing."

Ivy looks behind her before we turn a corner. "What the hell did he say to you?"

Shaking my head again, I repeat, "Nothing. It's nothing. I'm fine."

"Oh come on, Avery. He said something to set you off. What was it so I can go kick his ass?"

Of course she would. She'd go to bat for me under any circumstance, just like I would for her. We protect each other at all costs. It's how we've always been, and it'll never change for as long as we are joined at the hip.

I push the door open, and we're greeted with an unusually warm fall day. I take a deep breath and blow it out slowly as we cross onto the sidewalk. I ignore the weird looks I'm getting because my face is probably tear-stained and head in the direction of our apartment. Spanish was the last class of the day, thankfully. What I'm not so thankful about is that I barely have any notes on my Word doc. I couldn't concentrate with him sitting beside me. I barely comprehended what the professor said, so I was just writing random things that he stated, and I'm one-hundred percent positive my notes make zero sense. I'll have to ask Ivy to borrow hers.

When I say nothing, she softly asks, "Did he hurt your feelings?"

I shake my head. "No, just the opposite."

"I'm confused." She frowns. "Why are you crying then?"

"Ugh," I cry out to the sky as we stop at a crosswalk. Thankfully, no one is around to hear us or to see me continue to fall apart. "Because he gets under my skin and makes me believe things that I've been told otherwise."

She takes my hand in hers, and we cross the street. Once we're on the other side, she asks, "Things like what?"

"That I'm beautiful."

Chuckling under her breath, she says, "That's because you are."

I roll my eyes. "Maybe I once was, but that's not how I see myself anymore." Hell, I spend a good amount of time looking at my old photos of when I was skinny, comparing them to the photos I recently took of myself. I see the difference. My face is rounder, my shoulders wider, and my boobs far bigger.

"Look," she says as we enter the parking lot of our apartment. "If Reid Rathe is chasing after you—because that is what he's doing, right?" I nod and then shrug. She continues, "Reid doesn't date, Avery. If he likes you, that means something."

"Shouldn't that be a red flag then? If he doesn't date?"

"No...why would you say that about him?" Her tone is defensive, but her hand in mine gives an encouraging squeeze.

I throw my free hand in the air. "Because he's the guy I slept with and who snuck out the morning after Dustin's last party."

"Oh," she whispers. "Well, it's not a red flag."

"How could it not be?" I grind out. Sighing, I soften my tone because I shouldn't be taking my fears out on my best friend. She doesn't deserve that sort of treatment. "He doesn't date. He slept with me and snuck out the next morning. Two red flags. And..."

"And what?" she presses.

"He sometimes reminds me of Neil."

Reaching for our building's door, she pauses with her hand on the doorknob and turns a frown in my direction. "How?"

I let go of her hand and remove hair that snuck its way into the crease of my lips when a big gust of wind whipped it about. "Remember how obsessed I was with him?" She nods. "It's the same with Reid. And he's attractive. And fit. And charming." I grasp the knob for her and open the door for us to enter. As we climb the stairs, I continue. "It just feels so familiar, this feeling."

I put my key into our door and enter the apartment with Ivy hot on my heels. We drop our bags on the table, and she follows me into the kitchen. When I grab a glass for water, she leans against the counter with her arms across her chest and her eyes narrowed. I watch her while I drink, waiting for her to speak, but she doesn't.

"What?" I ask, setting my cup in the sink and wiping my mouth with the back of my hand.

"He is *not* Neil, Avery."

"You don't know that," I say, matching her stance.

"I do. I've known him for two years. For one, Dustin wouldn't be best friends with a loser. And two, all your red flags are just paranoia. He doesn't date because he's careful about who he picks to keep in his life. His family has a lot of money, and girls tend to flock to him because of it. Well, that, and he's kinda hot if you hadn't noticed."

"Oh, I've noticed."

She curtly nods. "He probably snuck out because he had somewhere to be. He, Dustin, and Jacob work out every morning. I'd bet every dollar I make this week in tips that he didn't sneak out for all the reasons you keep telling yourself. He's not that kind of guy, and let me tell you one other thing: He does not sleep around."

"So what?" I laugh. "Am I special or something? Am I supposed to believe that?"

She throws her hands into the air. "You're impossible. That's exactly what I'm saying, Avery. He doesn't sleep around, yet he chose you. Did you ever think he's attracted to you the same as your attracted to him?"

"Well, I already knew that."

"Then what's the problem?"

"Like I said: It feels familiar, and I don't want my heart hurt again. I don't think I'm capable of going through that again, of having him wise up someday and see that I'm exactly what he doesn't want and then destroying me like Neil did." My voice crackles at the end with emotion, but I shove it down with a clearing of my throat.

She sighs and her shoulders deflate. "I guess he'll just have to convince you otherwise."

I nibble on my bottom lip, feeling a little hopeless. "Yeah, I guess so."

"You're not going to make this easy on him, are you?"

I shrug a little. "I came out here to change my life. If he's going to fit into it, if he's going to break down the walls I built to protect myself, then no, I'm not going to make it easy. I can't. I promised myself I wouldn't."

She considers me for a moment then pulls me into a hug. She tucks her chin into my shoulder and says, "You know I love you, but you're so damn stubborn."

CHAPTER 10
REID RATHE

"ARE you sure your parents aren't going to mind that I'm tagging along?" Dustin asks. He's sitting in my passenger seat, playing a bubble shooter game on some app that he's become obsessed with the last few days. Thankfully, he can still hold a conversation while playing it.

I hadn't planned on going to meet my parents after school, but when they call, I answer. So, after working out with Dustin, I invited him along. He had nothing better to do tonight, so he had agreed.

The sun is three-quarters through the sky, and the leaves that have already fallen are being pushed across the road by a slight breeze. It'd be pretty if I didn't have this terrible feeling in my stomach about seeing them and what they could possibly want with me this time.

"It's just golf. They're not going to care," I say as we head out of the city where the traffic is lighter and the road is curvier.

He flicks his attention to me for only a moment before he's back to his phone. "Yeah, but the last time I met them, I got the feeling that they didn't like me much."

I snort. "They don't like most people."

"Ha!" he chirps. "Unless they have buckets of money, right? Man, did the apple fall far from the tree."

I scrub the back of my neck. "Yeah, I guess it did."

"What do they want anyway?"

Shaking my head, I stop at a useless stop sign. "I have no idea."

He fist-bumps the roof of my car when he wins a level of his game. "They didn't tell you anything?"

I shake my head. "They usually don't. But there's always an agenda to it, so I'm sure we'll find out soon enough."

Dustin pockets his phone in his gym shorts and settles into a slouch in the seat. "Maybe they just want to see how you're doing in classes or something."

"They could have just asked that question on the phone. Hell, they could have just contacted the school and talked to the professors." I wouldn't put it past them. They did it a lot last year just to make sure I was getting better grades than the year before. The year I was dating my ex and sort of went off-road with the energy of the relationship. It was a toxic relationship, and they knew it. Hell, even Dustin knew she was just after my family's money.

Despite my good grades last year, after the breakup and the fallout and the depression that Dustin had to pull me out of, I got my shit together, but they still don't fully trust me.

"God, your parents are so controlling. I don't know how you do it."

I shrug. "I grew up with it. I didn't know there was anything else until I met your family."

He turns a smirk in my direction. "I'm sure my parents would adopt you if you divorced yours."

I snort. "Funny," I say as we pull into the golf course parking lot.

Once the car is in Park, we climb out and head into the building in search of my parents. They told me they'd meet me inside, and as soon as we are in, we head right to the bar. That's where they always are when I meet them here. My mother has an addiction to wine and sits down to have a glass at any high-end bar she finds. Let's not mention how many glasses she has at home. I'd hate to know how much they spend on wine every year.

We find them immediately and slide into stools beside them, Dustin on my right, my mom on my left, and my father on her left. They're laughing at something and don't immediately notice us until I clear my throat.

My mother turns in my direction with a startled expression. "Darling," she greets warmly.

"Mom, Dad." My father nods at me in greeting.

Abandoning her glass of wine, she bends forward and presses the side of her lips to my cheek. Wrinkling her nose, she pulls away. "You smell like sweat. And what are you wearing?" she adds with a hiss. "This is no place for gym clothes."

Dustin and I are still wearing our cutoff shirts and gym shorts. I peek down at them with a frown.

Deciding not to care, I shrug, though it bothers me that they really care. It's always about the image. "We came from the gym. If you wanted us here on time, we didn't have time to change."

Blinking, finally realizing I didn't come alone, she looks over my shoulder at Dustin. Dustin gives her a small wave, and she plasters on a fake smile. "Hello," she greets. It's as genuine as the smile and makes me want to sigh. For once, can't she be human? Dustin is my best friend, for shit's sake. He's not going anywhere anytime soon. Even when we're done with college, he'll still be by my side. Nothing will change that.

"I'm not really good at golfing," Dustin begins to warm the conversation. "But I'm sure I can catch on fast."

"Oh," my mom says, grabbing her drink once more and taking a sip. "We won't be golfing. We're meeting the Kenzy family here."

My spine snaps straight. "And you invited me for...?"

She places a hand on my arm. "According to the Kenzys, you haven't been getting to know their Dorothy. Do you share any classes?"

I roll my eyes as Dustin shifts uncomfortably. He knows about my sort of arranged marriage with Dorothy, and he knows that I didn't really care about it even though it had pissed him off when I dropped that bomb with nothing but a shrug. "She's in a completely different major than I am. I doubt art school and medical school would share any classes."

She pouts. "Oh, come now, Darling. You could at least buy her lunch every now and then."

Looking down at the bar top, I flex my jaw. This isn't what I want anymore, and I didn't plan on having this conversation with them so soon, but..."I'm not buying her lunch, Mom."

"And why not?"

I snap my gaze back to hers. "Because I'm not marrying her."

She whips back as if she's been slapped. She has no idea I found someone else, and she won't know until the day I decide to tell her, which isn't today. She has no idea that there's someone in my life that I want to get to know and can't do it if I'm promised to another. I want to do this right by Avery. And the last thing I want is to lead Dorothy on. She's a nice girl and all that, but she's not who I want.

"What do you mean?" my dad asks. Dustin shifts at his tone. This has to be awkward for him, but truth be told, I'm glad he came along. He needs to know that I'm no longer interested in doing what my parents want for me anymore.

"I mean that it's my life, and I'm not going to marry someone you have set out for me."

"Nonsense," my mother says, laughing as if what I said was the greatest joke in the world. It makes me want to get up and leave, but I was taught better than that. I was taught respect, and even though my parents are the way they are, I'm still going to respect them.

Dustin clears his throat and coughs into his hand. "I think he's being serious, Mrs. R."

Her laughter dies down, and she looks at Dustin long enough to make him realize that he probably should have kept his mouth shut. "Don't," I hiss at her before she can say something stupid to him, something that will make him feel lesser than her. She can be petty like that sometimes, even if it's in the most polite manner.

She flicks her gaze back to me. "This is already all been arranged, Reid. The Kenzys are expecting you to marry their daughter once you're both out of college. They're looking forward to it, in fact. I'm sure their daughter is too."

I roll my eyes.

"Don't roll your eyes at me, Reid Romaine Rathe."

"Sorry, but I seriously doubt Dorothy is going to care. She hasn't even made an effort to get to know me. In fact, I haven't even seen her since school started."

"Maybe she's shy," my father chimes in.

My mother nods. "She's always been so shy to approach you at our parties. I bet that's it. You're just going to have to approach her."

I shake my head. "I'm not approaching her for anything other than being her friend."

I look over her head when I see familiar faces entering the room. Mrs. Kenzy's eyes land on mine, and a big smile takes over her face. Mr. Kenzy looks as grumpy as he always does, and Dorothy, who is fiddling with her hands nervously, follows her parents dutifully as they make their way to us.

"Ah, there you are," my mother says as they approach. She and Mrs. Kenzy peck each other's cheeks.

"Sorry we're late," Mrs. Kenzy says. "Dorothy's study group ran late."

At the mention of her name, Dorothy's eyes slide to mine. She's a pretty girl. She doesn't wear too much makeup, and her red hair is always tidy. She doesn't dress like a college girl though. With her pencil skirt and light blue blouse, she dresses like her mother still picks out her clothes. My father is right about her being shy. As quick as she looks at me, she looks quicker at her feet.

"This just got real awkward," Dustin whispers in my ear.

"Reid," my mother says with a forced smile. "Aren't you going to say hi to Dorothy?"

I clear my throat. "Hey," I manage.

Her gaze flicks back to mine, and when her mother nudges her shoulder, she straightens her back and grows a little bit of a spine. "Hi, Reid. How are you?"

"Good," I answer. This is stupid. I try not to, but that one word comes out as being anything but interested in having a conversation with her. Any other time, if our parents hadn't said we were to marry one another, this would be a good opportunity to talk with a friend, someone I grew up with, but now…

It's hard to sit here.

"How are your classes this year?" Mrs. Kenzy asks me.

"Fine," is my only answer.

"Do you guys want to grab a table while we catch up with your parents?" she asks, her face hopeful.

Yeah, that's not going to happen.

"Actually," I say as I stand up. "We were just leaving."

My mother frowns. "So soon?"

"Lots of studying to do," Dustin answers with humor in his tone as he stands up with me. I knew bringing him along would come in handy. While I hadn't anticipated him being my backup, that's exactly the role he decides to take.

I hug my mom around the shoulders, and in her ear, I whisper, "Remember what I said. I'm not marrying her."

She stiffens in my grasp but doesn't say anything. Probably because the Kenzys are here, and she doesn't want them to know what I've proclaimed. Knowing her, she'll probably try to make this work despite my protests. But I won't have it. I want to date Avery, and I can't do that with Dorothy chained to my future.

I shake my father's hand and say farewell to the Kenzy family, and then Dustin and I are leaving the golf course. Dorothy looked slightly put off that I'm leaving, but I can't do anything about that.

Fresh air greets us outside, and Dustin says nothing to me as we get in the car and drive away. But that all changes once the golf course is in the rearview mirror.

"Man, that was awkward as hell. Is that why you brought me along? To endure the shit show with a friend?"

"Sorry," I grumble under my breath, holding my steering wheel a little too tightly.

"No, it's fine. I get it."

"If I would have known—"

"I said it's fine, Reid." He blows out a breath. "I thought the last time I met them and your mother pretended I didn't exist was hard enough. This topped the cake."

"Yeah," I murmur, my mind reeling.

"That Dorothy girl was into you though. She was checking out your muscles." He pokes my pec, and I slap his hand away.

"She'll find someone else if she is."

"You're really not going to marry her?"

I shake my head.

"What changed?" he asks, his tone serious.

Glancing at him for a second, I decide how to answer him. There's no real way to tell him the truth.

My silence must speak volumes because he sighs. "This is about that girl you slept with, isn't it?"

I shrug.

"Sarah, right? Have you seen her since that night?"

I nod, deciding to give him truths to the questions I can answer. "We share a class."

"And?" he presses. "How did it go? Does she like you as much as you like her?"

I nod again. "Though she refuses to admit it. She thinks I'm too much like her ex."

He laughs out loud. "You have your work cut out for you then."

Rubbing my forehead, I answer, "Yeah, I sure do. And I have no idea what to do."

"Just keep after her, man. She'll come around."

God, I hope so. I didn't just stand up to my parents for nothing. If only she could see how serious I am about her.

CHAPTER 11
AVERY MOORE

I ALL BUT flop down onto the couch, my backpack slumping to the floor between me and the coffee table. I'm exhausted, and all I want to do is sleep for the next century.

My last class of the day was Spanish, and again, Reid sat next to me. Okay, so maybe it gave me the tingles that he chose me over his friend. But it shouldn't. Traitorous body. Traitorous heart.

For the entire first half of the lesson, he was sending me messages through a Word doc, same as before. I tried not to respond, to remain strong in my conviction, but he knew what buttons to push to get me to say something in return. I get it. He wants to get to know me. But I don't think he understands the magnitude of how much I'm afraid to get to know him.

Jacob ended up sitting next to Ivy for the class, leaving the two of us in our own little bubble. It was hard to breathe without smelling him. I'd love to know what he wears, or even if he wears anything at all because I could bottle that up and sell it for millions. It made it hard to concentrate on the professor, even when we weren't talking in our new method, when we were actually trying to pay attention and take notes.

Every movement he made had me keenly aware of him. His long fingers typing notes. His powerful chest heaving when he sighed because the professor got long-winded. The way he leaned forward to read something the professor put on the whiteboard and his muscles stretched against his shirt.

There was a moment when our legs brushed, and although we had jeans keeping our skin from touching, the contact lit up my nerves. I was on edge and turned on at the same time for the entire hour, and when we parted ways, him going to…wherever he goes after Spanish, and me going to the apartment, exhaustion settled in.

Wisely, Ivy didn't say a word the entire way home. But now?

I peep open an eye to see where she went, but she's still standing next to the door. Her arms are crossed over her chest, and a look of annoyance pinches her features.

A lecture is coming. I can see it all over her expression. It's practically her aura.

Before she can get going, I try a ploy tactic that has never worked in the past, but I've never stopped trying: A subject change before the subject can even be brought up. "Are you working tonight?"

One of her eyebrows rises, and I frown. I wish I could do that. "No, but seriously, Avery?"

I groan and cover my eyes. "Don't start."

She crosses the room, lifts my feet, and plops down on the couch, settling my feet back on her lap and patting my leg. "I feel for you, girl. This can't be easy. I honestly don't know how you're resisting him, but"—she sighs dramatically—"you two would make an adorable couple."

"No. Stop it." I point at her. "No adorable coupling."

She giggles. "What did you two talk about anyway?"

"A never-ending quiz on all my favorite things on the planet."

"And?" she asks.

I frown again. "And what?"

"And did you spend the entire time answering, or did you ask questions too?"

I blush and look away. "He may have given me his answers to the same questions." It was hilarious when he told me his favorite flower was a dandelion. I didn't have the heart to remind him that the dandelion was a weed, mostly because the dandelion reminded me of me. Unwanted. Easily destroyed. And then it reminded me of him. Persistent. Pretty.

A bright grin spreads across her cheeks. "That's kind of adorable."

I run a hand over my face. It was. I'll never admit it to Ivy, but I soaked up everything he told me about himself. Honestly, I feel kind of bad that I didn't ask a single question, but he never really gave me a moment to think of one before he popped another question.

"Let's talk about something else," I murmur behind my hand. "What are you doing tonight if you're not scheduled to work?"

She squeezes my leg. "Dustin and I were going to grab some supper together."

"That's nice."

"Want to come?"

"No." Being a third wheel is fun and all, but I'll pass.

"Oh, come on," she hisses. "All you've done is study since you arrived. Come hang out with me and your brother."

I drop my hand back to the couch cushion and glare at her. She's already texting on her phone, no doubt to

Dustin about the extra body that will be sitting next to their romantic bubble in a few hours. His response is almost immediate because her phone vibrates, and her face lights up. She holds the phone out for me and waves it in my face. "See? He doesn't care."

"Do I have to?" I whine.

"Yes!"

"Fine," I grumble. "Where are we going?"

"Sicily," she says, placing her phone on the arm of the couch next to her elbow. "It's a new Italian restaurant downtown. You'll love it."

"Is it expensive?" I ask, narrowing my eyes at her. All of us are in college, and funds are monitored closely. Or they should be anyway. At my last college, a lot of people dropped out because they no longer had the money to support themselves. I told myself I'd never be that person. I have the income from that calendar picture, and I have it budgeted out to last me until I have my brand-spankin'-new degree. Ivy, on the other hand, lives paycheck to paycheck.

She shakes her head. "We tried it out with my family when it first opened. It's not unaffordable. Trust me."

"All right," I sigh out. I do love pasta—if my figure is anything to go by. With no excuses left, I pull my legs off Ivy and sit up.

"Where are you going?" she asks as I pick up my backpack and stand.

"To study before I get ready for tonight." I head toward the hallway, shoulders slumped.

"Wear something cute tonight!" she hollers when I reach my room.

I do as she asked and put on a flowing black dress that does wonders to hide my hideous curves. It's the reason I bought it. The girl in the fitting room at the store told me so, and that was all I needed to hand over my card in the checkout line. That was right after the Neil situation, and I was desperate to feel pretty again. I may or may not have gone on a shopping spree that day, but thankfully, my parents covered the cost. They understood and put the money in my account the next day.

Spinning in the mirror, I get a good look at the backside. It *does* make my ass look fantastic. And my makeup is totally on point; not too much, but it highlights my cheeks and my eyes and makes my face look thinner.

A knock sounds at my door. I stride to it and open it to find an impatient Ivy with her arms crossed and her foot tapping. She's been checking in periodically, constantly reminding me of the time but also helping me curl my hair into soft beach waves. I'm not entirely thrilled about going, so I took my time, but now, I can hear a voice in the living room, and I wish I wasn't the one everyone was waiting on.

"Dustin's here," she says, then she gives me a once-over. "You look gorgeous, girl."

I do a little curtsy. "Thanks."

"Ready?" I nod and she hesitates before she whispers, "Don't kill me."

I scowl. "Why would I kill you?"

She grimaces and looks down the hallway. "Just... remember that you love me."

She takes off down the hall, and I follow her, a needle of fear in my heart. What did she do?

As soon as we enter the living room, I stop dead in my tracks. Standing and talking with Dustin is Reid. My heart stutters and leaps with joy before I stomp it down quickly. I may be excited that he's standing in my apartment, looking fine as hell, but he can't be here.

He's dressed in a black, long-sleeve, buttoned-down shirt that's rolled up at the sleeves, showing off his tan, muscled arms. His dark blue jeans hug every part of his hips and thighs, and his hair is styled in its usual carefree way. There's a slight stubble along his jaw that was there today in class, and it's extremely appealing on him.

I look at Ivy and take in her guilty expression. "Is this a double date?" I accuse, my cheeks flaming hot.

My brother laughs out loud. "Absolutely not." He slaps Reid on the shoulder. "He knows better than to date my sister."

I frown at Reid's sneaky smile but ask Dustin, "Then what's he doing here?"

He shrugs. "I invited Reid when Ivy asked if you could come along. Figured we could make it a thing."

I fidget under the weight of Reid's stare, almost daring me to tattle on him and tell Dustin that, despite his wishes, Reid is pursuing me. But I'm not an asshole, and I can turn Reid away myself. If I want to. I definitely want to.

Ivy claps her hands together once, interrupting the silence that was probably awkward for everyone but me and Reid, and says, "Shall we?"

Dustin snakes his arm around Ivy's waist and leads her to the door. "You got reservations, right?"

"Yep," she confirms, popping the 'p.' "Table for four."

"Who's driving?" I ask as they head out the door. Reid and I are still rooted to our spots, the space charging between us the farther and farther Dustin and Ivy get away.

"Dustin," Ivy calls over her shoulder.

As soon as they're in the hallway, Reid returns his gaze to me. He holds it for a few heartbeats.

"What?" I ask quietly when he stares too long.

"You look beautiful," he whispers.

I blush and look down at my heels. "You can't say things to me like that tonight."

"If you gave me your number, I could text them to you."

I look at him from under my lashes. "Not going to happen."

He shrugs and crosses the distance between us. I can't help the shiver that travels down my spine when he leans and whispers, "I'll get it eventually, Avery. And then I'll text you all the things you won't let me say out loud."

Leaving me speechless, he heads out into the hallway. I stand there for a few minutes, trying to get my body to cool down. He makes it so hard to resist him because my body absolutely betrays me, especially when he's close to me. It's difficult not to give him what he wants, not to break down my barriers and be the person he sees me as.

I take a deep breath, grasp the keys off of the table, and lock up the apartment. As soon as I'm out to Dustin's car, I find Dustin starting the engine with Ivy in the front seat and Reid sitting in the back. It probably would have made more sense for Reid to sit up front with Dustin, but I can't help but feel that Ivy did this on purpose. I plan to kick her ass later. Or, at the very least, give her the silent treatment until the morning.

I hop into the back seat next to Reid, who flashes me a bright smile. "No funny business," I whisper to him.

He holds his hands up in surrender, and Dustin, unaware of our brief exchange because he's deep in conversation with Ivy, pulls out of the parking lot, and we head off campus.

For the first ten minutes, I stare out the window, trying to forget the devilishly handsome guy sitting next to me. I put minimal effort into the conversation the three of them are having and, instead, watch as the fall leaves swoosh into the air upon our passing.

I startle when something touches my thigh, however. Glancing down, I see Reid's hand, his knuckles brushing back and forth on my bare thigh. I raise my gaze to his, but he's pretending not to pay attention to me. I'm not stupid though, I know he's completely aware that his fingers are touching me and that he's completely aware that Dustin can't see it in the rearview mirror.

Frowning, I grab his hand and try to set it aside, but he wraps his hand around my fingers and holds on tight. My frown deepens every time I try to pull my hand away, but eventually, I sigh, giving in. My body slackens against the seat, and he takes that as a cue to fold his fingers between mine.

My heart flutters as I stare at our joined hands. I should stop this. It'll give him the wrong impression. Hell, it's giving me the wrong impression. But his hand is warm and calloused and fits perfectly around mine, and…I like it. I shouldn't, but I do.

Ivy turns around in her seat and asks, "How did studying go?" She then looks at our joined hands and winks at me, a gleeful look in her eyes.

"Fine," I bite out. This is her fault. She could have at least warned me. Hell, she could have sat back here with me. Now I'm holding the hand of a man I'm extremely attracted to, one who is trying to…date me? Screw me? I don't even know anymore.

"Is this it?" Dustin asks, pointing to a brick building. I look around. I hadn't even realized we were downtown yet.

Ivy turns back around and looks where he points. "Yes! There, right there, there's a parking spot." She claps her hands together when he slides the car into it and puts it into Park.

I let go of Reid's hand quickly and exit the car. The wind swirls around me, and I breathe it in deep, trying to calm my nerves, and then I head inside with the others.

The restaurant looks expensive with muted cream tones and black tablecloths, but when we sit down, order our drinks, and look at the menu, I see that it isn't half bad. Easily affordable and, by the smells surrounding us, yummy too.

While we wait for our food, Ivy keeps the conversation flowing. She's sitting next to me, thank God, because I don't know if I could take another minute sitting next to Reid. My body is already shot from the car ride.

That doesn't stop Reid from stealing glances in my direction. We keep catching each other's gaze, and every time, it makes me blush. There's something in his eyes that lets me know that he may be talking with my brother, but he's certainly paying attention to everything I'm doing.

I lean toward Ivy and whisper, "You could have warned me."

"Then you wouldn't have come."

"You're right, I wouldn't have," I hiss. "But you think you're cupid now, don't you?"

She pats my thigh. "Don't be mad. This is good for you."

I close my eyes and rub my temples, and when I open them, it's to find concern etched on Reid's face. "Are you feeling okay?" he asks.

Abruptly, I stand up. I need to get out of here, get away from his stare for just a few minutes. "Yes, I'm fine. I'm just—I'm going to go use the bathroom."

"Do you want me to come with you?" Ivy asks, taking the napkin off of her lap and setting it on the table.

I touch her shoulder as I get ready to pass her and head to the bathroom. "I'll be fine."

I all but rush to the bathroom, and once I'm inside, I shut the door and lean against it. Taking several deep breaths, I work like hell to calm my heart. It's easier in here, surrounded by toilet paper and soap, to have a little perspective.

"It's simple, Avery," I tell myself. "Just be straight with him and ask him to stop advancing on you."

Even I know that's a lie. It's not that simple. Not anymore, not with how charming he is and how much he makes my body light on fire and my heartbeat race so fast that I can't catch my breath sometimes.

I head to the sink, wet my hands, and run them over my neck to cool down my skin. I look in the mirror as I do it, seeing the panic set in my expression. Every barrier I set up in place is trying to crumble down, and I feel like I'm holding it all up with off-brand tape that isn't sticky enough.

I grip the sink and lean closer to myself. "You can do this. Just have dinner, go home, and crawl into bed."

Easy.

With some courage in my spine, I head out of the bathroom, but as soon as I'm in the hallway, I come to an abrupt halt. Reid is there, leaning against the wall, clearly waiting for…me.

"You okay?" he murmurs.

"I'm fine."

He rights himself from the wall and touches my cheek. "You look pale."

A soft breath leaves my lips. I don't mean to, but I lean ever so slightly into his touch. "You can't touch me like that."

"Like what?"

"Like this," I say, waving my hand at his still brushing my face. "And you certainly can't look at me the way you're looking at me tonight."

He grins a little. "Like what?"

"Like you've seen me naked and want another round."

His grin widens, and he turns me until my back is against the wall. He braces one hand beside my head and says, "But I have seen you naked."

I sigh and look at his chest. "What do you want from me, Reid, really?"

"I think we should exchange numbers."

I shake my head and laugh a little. "In your dreams."

He's quiet for so long that I look back up at him. His expression is serious as he whispers, "You don't trust me, do you?"

"No."

"Why?"

"Because you don't seem to be the commitment type," I say even though I'm beginning to think I'm wrong about that. He's sure committed to pursuing me.

"You barely know me, how would you know?"

I look away.

"That's what I thought."

He gets close to me and runs his nose across my jaw. My skin is lit on fire from the intimate touch, and my hands immediately land on his narrow hips to keep from swaying. "What do I want from you?" he whispers. "I don't know, but I'm interested in you. I can't get you off of my mind. You're all I think about. Do I want to have sex with you again? Yes, because you're hot, Avery. But I'm way more interested in the girl than I am about sex."

I gulp and lie my ass off. "I'm not interested."

"A lie," he says, calling me out. "Tell me why you're lying. Does this have to do with your last relationship?"

I freeze.

He pulls his nose away from my jaw and searches my eyes. "I don't know the details, but I know you got hurt.

I'm not him, Avery. Please believe me when I tell you that. I don't sleep around, and I wouldn't be coming onto you so hard if I didn't believe we'd be good together."

I shake my head. "The other week contradicts that, the whole one-night stand thing."

"Because you fell into my arms, and then I got a look at those fucking eyes, and I was done for. Sucked in. And then you invited me back to your place."

"Yeah, and then you left. That doesn't sound like someone who is interested in more than just sex."

He sighs a little. "I work out with your brother every morning. Besides, I didn't want you to be upset that I was still there when you woke up. I didn't want you to have to feel awkward."

"Thoughtful of you," I murmur sarcastically.

He smirks. "I'm a thoughtful guy, something you'd know if you gave me your number."

"Not happening," I breathe out because he's looking at my lips. His own lips part, drawing my attention, and his breath fans my face on a slow exhale.

"You want to kiss me, don't you, Avery?"

I bite my bottom lip and look away again. Crooking a finger under my chin, he tips my face back to his. Gently, carefully, he presses his lips to mine, and god, if it isn't everything I could ever wish for and more. Definitely more. It's searing straight into my soul and makes my toes curl.

He opens his mouth a little and brushes his tongue along my bottom lip, and I open for him, letting his tongue sweep against mine. A few more swipes and he's pulling away, leaving me breathless.

Leaning his forehead against mine, he says, "I'm not the only one who is interested. I'm not the only one who feels the pull to the other. Don't pretend otherwise,

Avery. You know we'd be good together if you could just wrap your head around giving another guy a chance."

And with that, he leaves, turning down the hall and heading back to the table.

CHAPTER 12
REID RATHE

TODAY'S CLASSES were long and grueling, and now that it's over, there's an extra drag in my step. Dustin, Jacob, and I are headed to Dustin's apartment, and the thought of being so close to her is killing me.

The other night, when I returned to the table, Dustin was completely unaware. Ivy, on the other hand, knew exactly what I was doing. She knew I was going after Avery, but besides giving me a long, hard stare, she said nothing. I really am going to have to owe her for keeping my secret from her boyfriend.

Not going to lie, the lie itself is near torture, especially when I hang out with Dustin all the time. He knows I'm going after a girl, but he has no idea that it's his sister. I can't tell him either. Lord knows what he'd do if he ever found out that I had her pinned against the wall only a couple of days ago while he sat unaware at a nearby table. That's one friendship I don't plan on losing, and it would surely be in jeopardy if he ever found out.

I have no idea what this means in the long term. Especially if Avery ever decides to give in and date me, because he will find out eventually. Hopefully, by then,

I'll have a plan to drop the news carefully. Who knows, maybe Dustin will change his mind by then.

We pass by the courtyard, and Jacob tugs us in the direction of the taco hut. "You're hungry *again*?" Dustin says, exasperated. "Dude, seriously, we just ate two hours ago."

He lets go of our elbows, and I say, "He's always hungry. Just be thankful it's not your fridge he's raiding."

Dustin chuckles as Jacob slides up to the counter and orders two tacos. He turns to us, his wallet out. "Want any?"

Dustin and I cross our arms and shake our heads. "Some of us don't have bottomless stomachs."

"It's not bottomless." Jacob scowls as he's handed his tacos. "It just empties quickly. It's called a high metabolism."

I point at him. "I don't want to hear it when you can't squeeze your ass into your jeans anymore."

Jacob swivels to look at his backside. "It's a nice ass though, isn't it?"

Dustin shoves him, nearly knocking the tacos right out of Jacob's grip. "It'll have its own orbit soon."

Jacob, unoffended, unwraps a taco and takes a bite, grinning around a mouthful of food. "The chicks dig it. Just last night—"

Dustin and I groan, cutting him off. Tightening the straps of my backpack while spinning and walking backward, I say, "We don't need to hear about your fling. You talk about her enough as it is. Your sex life with her isn't an image I want in my head, especially if it involves your ass."

I turn around and bump into someone. They teeter to the side, and I snatch out my hands and grip their shoulders to keep them from falling over. "Sorry," I immediately say. The girl looks up and pushes the hair from her face. "Dorothy? Oh man, I'm so sorry. I didn't see you there."

Releasing her shoulders, I step back, directly in the center of Dustin and Jacob.

"Dorothy?" Jacob whispers in my ear. "*The* Dorothy? Dude, she's kinda hot. In a nerdy sort of way."

I glare at him. "She can hear you."

Jacob cringes and looks back at Dorothy. "Sorry."

Fiddling with her fingers, she shrugs. "It's okay."

I frown at her. "No, it's not. You don't have to be nice to him."

"Everyone's nice to me. I'm just that guy," Jacob defends.

I rake a hand over my face. There's no helping him. Instead of giving him the attention he wants, I turn it to Dorothy. "I haven't seen you around campus."

"Yeah," she says, clearing her throat. The awkwardness is so thick that Dustin starts chuckling. "I haven't seen you either."

I shrug. "Always on the go, I guess."

She nods. "Me too."

We stand there for a few unbearable moments, saying nothing, until I ask, "Are you going to class or going home?"

"Home."

As far as I know, Dorothy is living with her parents. They wanted to keep their daughter close, but she has to have friends on campus, right? Maybe somewhere to escape? Study?

I point behind her. "The parking is over there."

"Oh," she says, attempting something that should sound like a giggle but comes out as a distressed goose. "Actually, I came over here hoping to bump into you."

Dustin elbows the frown off my face by hitting me in

the gut. "How long have you been waiting here?" Because she couldn't have known my class schedule.

"About a half hour," she admits with a shrug. "I tried yesterday but never saw you."

"Stalker much?" Jacob murmurs.

I shift to the other foot, ready to be done with the conversation but not sure how to end it. "What did you need from me?"

"I...um." She looks at Jacob and Dustin. "I was hoping we could talk."

"About what?"

"The other day, at the golf course." She pushes hair behind her ear and briefly glances at my feet.

I tense. "What about it?"

"Golf course?" Jacob asks. "You went golfing without me?"

"No, we never went golfing," I say, rolling my eyes.

"We?" Jacob fully turns to me and Dustin. "You both went?"

Dustin laughs. "It's not what you think, but it's one hell of a story. I'll tell you later."

"Thanks, guys," I grumble under my breath. "Ignore them," I add to Dorothy.

She flicks her gaze back to mine. "I just wanted to say that I'm sorry about our parents. I hope that...I hope they weren't too pushy with you."

"You and I both know that they were."

She nods slowly. "Yeah, my mom's been hounding me about talking to you at school."

"Why?" Jacob asks. Dorothy is clearly having a hard time talking to me as it is. I'm not a complete asshole, and I don't want to make her more uncomfortable.

I smack Jacob in the ribs. "Mind your own business."

"Can I ask you something?" Dustin asks her, butting in.

"Sure," she answers in a whisper.

"I know about the arranged marriage thing. Do you actually want to follow through with it?"

She shrugs and folds her arms around herself, and it's then that I know that she does. I don't know if it's out of convenience—because she's clearly not getting any dates or, hell, spending any time with men by how this conversation is going—or if it's because she follows her parents' word as law. But I have to figure out how to let her down gently. Maybe in private because doing so in front of my friends would be an asshole move.

I change the subject. "How are your classes this year?"

She brightens up a little. "A lot harder than I thought they'd be, but I like a challenge."

"That's good," I say, giving her a smile that makes her blush and pull on her fingers again.

"How about yours?"

"Can't complain." Actually, I can if the weight of my backpack is anything to go by. But I don't complain out loud because, honestly, I want this conversation to end.

Dustin takes pity on me and coughs into his hand. "We should get going."

"Yeah, we should." I squeeze Dorothy's shoulder. "It was nice seeing you."

"You too," she says as we pass her.

When we're out of earshot, Jacob starts to laugh. "That was the most awkward thing I've ever seen you wiggle out of."

"She's clearly into you," Dustin adds.

I grumble under my breath. "You two have no idea what it's like to be me."

"Why didn't you just tell her then and there that this arranged marriage is not going to happen?" Dustin asks.

"I didn't want to hurt her feelings in front of an audience."

"You're too nice," Jacob grumps. "Just do what I do."

"What? Sleep with her and then block her number the next day?" I'm being rude, but honestly, I don't need their input. I get enough of that from my parents.

Jacob throws his taco wrappers away in a nearby trashcan and sucks in a breath. "You wound me."

I sigh and nudge him with my shoulder. "Sorry. Just… this whole thing is pissing me off."

"Is this because of the girl you refuse to talk about?" Dustin asks.

Jacob grins knowingly. "Yeah, Reid. Is it?"

I give him the look to keep his mouth shut, and he turns his grin to the pavement, his body shaking with silent laughter as we head to the crosswalk.

"Someday, you'll have to introduce me to her," Dustin adds. "You can't keep hiding her forever. It's not like I'll steal her away from you or something. Ivy's a handful as it is."

I grip my backpack straps and press the button for the crosswalk. "Yeah, someday," I say nonchalantly. *If you don't find out and kill me first.*

CHAPTER 13
AVERY MOORE

"YOU HAVE way more detailed notes than I do," I say, looking over Ivy's printed-out notes for Spanish. She's highlighted a bunch of key topics for me, and I could just kiss her for that.

We're sitting on my bed, working on our latest Spanish assignment. A month of school and several assignments later and they don't get any easier.

She's still in her work clothes—black pants and black shirt—and she smells like buttermilk pancakes and syrup from the diner. When she walked through the door smelling like food, my stomach growled, but she revealed a take-home box full of pancakes and bacon, and we immediately dug in before getting to the homework.

"That's because you make goo-goo eyes with Reid the entire time."

"I do not make goo-goo eyes," I say under my breath.

She takes the notes from my hand. "Then what do you call it?"

I raise my gaze to hers after attempting to get the notes back and failing. "Friendly conversation."

She laughs. Tips her head back and belts out a laugh so loud it booms off my walls.

"So not funny," I say when she calms down and passes the notes back.

"So then tell me what happened when you two went to the bathroom at Sicily."

"I already told you. Nothing happened."

She slaps my thigh, and I hiss from the sting. "You two were gone for a long time. Longer than it takes to take a tinkle. I know he went there for you. Tell me what happened."

"No."

She grabs hold of my arm and tugs it to her chest. "Please?" she begs.

I rub my eyes and set my notes down. "He kissed me."

Gasping, she releases my arm and puts her hand over her heart. "How romantic."

Biting on the corner of my lip, I say, "Yeah, it kind of was." Every time I think of how he cornered me, my heart flutters. Neil never did anything like that.

"This has to be fun for you guys."

"What?"

She waves her hand in the air. "Sneaking around. The secrecy. The forbidden nature of the entire thing."

"We are *not* sneaking around. Nothing is happening between us," I lie.

She laughs again. "You so are and there so is. So did he just kiss you, or did you talk?"

I shrug a little and stack the papers on my knee. "We talked a little."

"So does this mean you're coming around to him?"

I shrug again. "I don't want to."

Her grin is broad. "But you are. God, you two. My heart can't take it."

"Don't get too excited. I won't even give him my number."

Her smile is replaced by a frown. "Why not?"

I sigh and flop back onto my pillow. "I'm just not there yet."

She pokes my ribs gently. "You know that if I could go back in time and murder Neil before you started dating, I would, right?"

Rolling my head to the side, I look her square in the eye and say, "I have no doubt."

"You'd have to strip down to your underwear and pose for another calendar to get my bail money."

I chuckle under my breath and wave at my body. "Nobody wants to see this."

A sly look overtakes her expression. "Reid does."

"Well, Reid isn't all there, then." I tap my temple in emphasis.

"Or he is, and you're just being a bitch to yourself. You do realize that you're the only one who sees your weight, right?"

"And Neil," I correct.

"Neil's a pussy."

I grin at her. "A total douche. Couldn't even find a clit if my pubic hair was in the shape of an arrow."

She cringes. "That takes a 'special' kind of man not to find it."

"Oh, he's special all right."

"Reid would give him a run for his money. Hell, he already has."

I sigh. "Whose side are you on here? Mine or Reid's?"

"Team Reid, obviously."

I flop an arm over my eyes. "Wonderful."

She digs her toes into my thigh. "You know I'm always on your side, but sometimes, I have to point out the obvious and tell you when you're being ridiculous.

This is one of those times. Give the poor man your number."

"Nope," I answer behind my arm.

"You're going to be the death of me," she whispers. "I swear to God, if I die before I see you two get together, I'm going to haunt your ass."

I chuckle under my breath and remove my arm from my face. "And if we never get together?"

She juts her chin. "Then I'll possess you."

"That's not creepy at all."

"I'll possess you and then force you to date Reid."

I raise my eyebrows at her. "You have this all planned out, don't you?"

"If it was possible to come back to life, I would have already done it by now."

I sigh. "I'll think about giving him my number." Because I know she'll hound me until I do. I like him. More than like him. He wasn't wrong when he said he knew I was interested. I'm just not at the number-giving phase yet. And to be honest, I'm enjoying the chase. I'm enjoying that he's working so hard to get me to give in to him. I just want to make sure it's not because he just wants to catch me instead of keep me. I'm not a small fish. There's no catch-and-release here. The next guy I date, I want to be sure I'm a keeper. You know, without the flaying part.

"That's all I ask."

I sit up and set my notes aside. "Am I to assume that I've killed the studying mood?"

"What did you have in mind?" she asks with a mischievous grin. "A party?"

"What? No!" Jesus, this apartment is my safe place. The last thing I want is a bunch of frat boys and girls with too-small dresses spilling beer on my walls and dry humping all over my couch.

"A walk?"

I shake my head. "I want something that helps me escape from my own thoughts."

She claps her hands and climbs off my bed. "A movie then."

I nod slowly. "That would work."

She claps again, her excitement almost contagious as I begin sliding my books back into my backpack. "I'll text Dustin and Reid. Get ready, chica. We're getting a huge bowl of popcorn."

"What? No! Not Reid!"

Her phone is already in her hand, but she pauses in the text to look up at me. "Relax. It's not a double date. Just friends. Besides, what moves could he possibly make sitting next to your brother?"

I frown as I think it over. "You have a point."

"See? Now shush. Go get ready." She exits my room as her fingers tap against her screen.

CHAPTER 14
REID RATHE

"HERE, MAN," Dustin says, passing me a bottle of beer.

"Thanks."

I check my watch and look out the window to the darkening sky. I haven't left Dustin's yet. I have Spanish homework to do, but I just don't feel like doing it. It's not due for a few days anyway, so I should be good. My notes are terrible though. They're intermixed with a conversation that Avery and I had. Weeding through them is going to be difficult without rereading our conversation until it's memorized more so than the notes themselves.

God, I'm pathetic.

Chasing after a girl who says she doesn't want me. The only thing keeping me going is knowing that, for a fact, she does. I'll break through her ice. I'll find the right thing to say or do at the right time. Somehow.

Footsteps stomp down the hallway, and I turn my attention there. Jacob and Dustin are in the living room with me, so that only leaves...

Dustin's roommate emerges from his room at the back

of the apartment and stops in the living room to stare with his hands on his hips.

Jacob looks up from his phone and grins. "Gary!"

"Drinking again," Gary grumbles as he takes us in and the bottle of beer in each of our hands.

Gary is exactly as I'd picture him if someone just told me his name. A true nerd. Glasses too big for his chubby-cheeked baby face, pimples dotting his stub nose, red hair that hasn't seen a pair of scissors in who knows how long, and a pathetic mustache. He spends hours playing video games in his room, hardly ever emerging.

He refuses to go to the parties and get to know some of our friends. If the person isn't gaming, Gary has no interest in them. And he doesn't drink. In fact, I'm positive he's called campus security on our parties a few times just to get the drunk folks gone so he could hear whatever came through that giant neon-blue headset of his.

The only reason I know about the headset is because we snuck into his room one day while he was in class just to see if he had porn magazines. It would have made him more likable if he had, but we came up empty-handed.

"Those plaid pants suit you well," I tease. "Really makes your chicken legs look like they have some muscle."

"Screw you, rich kid," Gary hisses.

I hold a hand over my heart. "Rude." It stung, but I'm not going to show him any weakness.

"You started it," he growls. "Always here with your sports car. Girls always want you because of your stupid messy hairstyle. Do you think you're perfect, Reid?" He hisses the last sentence, and it grates at my nerves.

"Of course I'm perfect," I say with a smile. "Otherwise, you wouldn't feel the need to point it out."

He sneers at me and looks at Dustin. "I don't know how you hang out with these two douchebags."

"Simple," Jacob says after taking a swig. "He's a douche too."

The three of us laugh, and Gary's face grows red as his hair with anger.

"Oh, what's wrong, Gary?" Jacob jokes. "Can't handle being out-douched?"

Gary throws up his hands. "I can't do this anymore."

Dustin comes down from laughing. "Do what?"

"Live here!" He slams his meaty hands back onto his hips. "I'm moving out. I came out here to tell you that, and as of right now, I know for certain it was the best move I've ever made in my life."

"So I'm assuming you haven't had sex before, then?" Jacob asks.

"Screw you," Gary says through clenched teeth before he starts stomping back down the hallway.

"Gary, wait!" Dustin says, but Gary doesn't listen. His door slams a few seconds later. "Fuck," he adds in a whisper.

"Is it such a bad thing?" Jacob asks. "Then we can have any party we want to at any time."

"Yes, it's a bad thing." Dustin rakes a hand through his hair. "I count on his half of the rent."

I twist my lips to the side. "So get another roommate."

He drops his hand to his lap. "I'll have to." He glances at me speculatively. "What about you?"

"What about me?"

"Move in with me."

I raise my eyebrows. "I already have an apartment."

He shrugs. "Give it up. Move in with me."

I take a good, long swig. My parents would hate it. "I don't know…"

"Come on," he begs. "That one girl you're after lives in the building, right? You could be closer to her."

"True," I murmur. I'd be right across the hall from her. It'd be harder to keep my secret from Dustin, but it would be easier to see her whenever I want to. "I don't know. I'll have to think about it."

"That's all I ask." He downs his beer and sets it on the coffee table. "So you're really not going to tell me about her? I could totally be your wingman since she lives in the building."

"No," I say firmly.

"He's just not ready yet," Jacob interjects, going back to his phone. At least he's not smirking knowingly.

"Wait, you know who she is?" Dustin asks.

Jacob only glances up for a second. "I may have an idea."

"Then tell me."

He tucks his chin and pinches his lips together. "That's not my story to tell."

"Since when do you not tell stories?" Dustin grumbles.

He only shrugs and goes back to his phone. "I can keep shit to myself."

"Sure, sure," Dustin gripes. He looks back at me. "You're really not going to tell me?"

I shake my head.

His sigh comes from deep within his chest. "We keep nothing from each other, man."

Guilt wafts through my entire body, making the beer in my stomach curdle. I rub at the back of my neck and slump against the couch. "Just give me time to sort this all out, and then I'll tell you." It's not a lie. Not a single lie in that promise and it eases some of the guilt.

He sighs and rolls his neck. "Fine. But I want the

details when you do. And don't go blabbing to Jacob first."

"Hey!" Jacob shouts, pretending to have hurt feelings.

Dustin places a hand over his heart. "I'm the best friend. The best man at his future wedding. You're the pet we keep around who eats everything in the apartment and humps anything he can find."

Jacob purses his lips. "Oddly accurate."

I chuckle under my breath. "At least you don't chew up shoes, and we don't have to watch you take a shit outside."

Jacob points the neck of his bottle at me. "That can be arranged."

I gag. "That's one image I didn't need to have in my head."

Dustin's phone chirps, and he digs it out of his pocket. He quickly reads it and then looks up at us. "Ivy and my sister want a movie night."

"Okay?" Jacob says, going back to his phone.

"They want us to drive them," Dustin amends.

"Pussy-whipped," Jacob mutters, never looking up from his phone.

"Says the man who hasn't stopped texting a girl since we got here," I interject, raising my eyebrows at him.

"How do you know it's a girl?" he asks.

I give him the look.

"Okay, fine. Whatever." He pockets his phone and stands. "You two go ahead. I'm not going."

Dustin takes our empty bottles of beer and heads to the kitchen with them. From there, he asks, "What the hell are you going to do instead?"

Jacob wiggles his eyebrows at me.

"He's going to go get laid," I answer for him.

He leaves while whistling, closing the door softly

behind him and leaving me with my own thoughts while Dustin cleans up.

"Are you sure you want me to come?" I shout to him.

He pops his head out of the kitchen, a frown pulling down his brows. "Why wouldn't I?"

I shrug. "I feel like I've been crashing your dates lately."

He shrugs and heads back into the kitchen. "My sister is coming too."

Butterflies flutter in my stomach, and I'm reminded of the restaurant where I pinned her against the wall and took her mouth. What I'd give to taste her one more time, but I don't know how I'm going to do that at a movie theater. I got lucky at Sicily.

"You should really get to know her," he adds.

Oh, I'm sure trying all right. But she's stubborn as hell. I can't tell him that though, so I ask, "Why?"

He heads out of the kitchen, drying his hands. "I want my best friend and my sister to be friends. Ivy will no doubt have her as her maid of honor at the wedding, and I want you as my best man. It would be nice if you both were on a good level of friendship."

I look down at my hands and nervously crack my knuckles. "There is no wedding, dude. You have to ask the question first."

I look up in time to see a smile spread across his face. "Oh, I plan to. I'm going to marry that woman."

"No second guesses?" He and Ivy have always been solid since I've known them. Even when they were at different points in their lives, they still stuck together. I want that…with his sister. The sister he wants me to be "friends" with.

He shakes his head. "She's who I want."

"You're a lucky man, then."

"How so?"

I rest my arm on the back of the couch. "Not everyone knows what they want. Not everyone finds who they want to spend the rest of their life with."

He must take that to mean something other than it's not because he crosses his arms. "You'll find your woman, too, Reid. And who knows, maybe it's this mysterious woman."

Trying hard to hide my smile because I'd want nothing more, I nod and stand from the couch. "Let's hope so."

"But you'll have to tell me who she is before the wedding."

I roll my eyes. "You'll know when she walks down the aisle."

He playfully shoves my shoulder as I slide past him and to the door. He follows me. "How much do you want to bet that it's a chick flick?"

"I won't be taking that bet," I say as I open the door and we step out into the hallway. He sounds disappointed, but honestly, if I'm sitting next to Avery, I don't care if we watch Barney.

CHAPTER 15
AVERY MOORE

"THANKS FOR DRIVING," Ivy tells Reid after we're given our movie tickets and head toward the concession stand. The smell of the popcorn is drawing me in with the promise of chewable distraction instead of who I wanted to chew on the entire drive here.

I sat next to Reid in the front seat of his elaborate, silver sports car while Dustin and Ivy filled the car with conversation from the cramped back seats. As much as I tried, I couldn't help but watch him drive. He was confident in the way he steered, and the car roared to life with a simple press of his foot on the pedal. He effortlessly glided the car through traffic, one strong hand on the steering wheel and the other resting dangerously close to my thigh.

Every now and then, he'd catch me looking at him and would wear the smuggest smirks that tingled my insides. I'd blush and look away, but my entire body was heated. Hell, it still is. The cold autumn air did nothing for it.

Ivy and Dustin get in line before us, and I'm keenly aware of Reid's body directly behind my back. We're almost touching, and every nerve in my body is lit, waiting for him to close that distance.

He leans a little, not enough to touch my backside but enough to purr into my ear, "Your hair smells amazing."

My cheeks redden, and I look down at my feet.

When I say nothing else, he adds, "And you look stunning in sweatpants."

I bite my bottom lip as butterflies kick up in my stomach and swirl around. Ivy and Dustin have no idea what he's saying to me. They're too wrapped up in their own little bubble to notice that Reid is most certainly hitting on me.

Popcorn and sodas in hand, Ivy and Dustin step to the side, giving us space to approach the counter. The clerk looks up, and I place my order. "A medium popcorn and a medium Diet Coke, please."

"Make that two of each," Reid says, pulling out his wallet from his back pocket.

I frown at him. "I can pay for myself."

"I know you can," he murmurs while pulling out cash. "But you don't have to."

"I'm a big girl, Reid. I'm capable of taking care of myself."

He hands over the money and lifts his eyebrows at me. "And I'm telling you that, when you're with me, I'll take care of you."

We hold each other's stare until our sodas and popcorn are laid out in front of us. I sigh and take mine. "Thank you."

"My pleasure," he says, picking up his drink and taking a sip.

"Ready?" Ivy asks as we meet them off to the side.

I nod, and she and Dustin turn on their heels and head toward our theater. Dustin, balancing their shared popcorn and his soda in one arm, grabs Ivy's hand and closes his fingers around hers. It's such a simple act, and I'm so happy for my brother that he's found someone to share little moments like these with.

We walk by a bathroom, and two skinny, dolled-up women do a double take at Reid. They lean into each other, whispering as they keep their eyes on him. Jealousy is an ugly thing, and that ugly thing is rearing its head. I shouldn't be jealous that other girls are ogling him. He's not mine after all.

Reid spares them a glance before he wraps his free arm around my shoulders and pulls me in close to his side. He presses a soft kiss to my hairline, and I don't miss the disappointment on the two girls' faces.

I hide my grin well when I say, "You're being mighty bold." I tip my head to Dustin.

"As far as he knows, I'm just being friendly."

"Is that so?" I ask, looking up at him. God, he's beautiful.

He curtly nods. "He told me as much before we came and got you girls."

"Oh?"

He smiles down at me. "He wants us to be friends."

I laugh under my breath. "He's going to kick your ass when he finds out."

Cringing, he replies, "Probably."

"And yet, that doesn't stop you."

He kisses my hairline again as we head into the darkness of the theater. Against my skin, he says, "Nothing is going to stop me, Avery."

I bite my bottom lip and pray to God that he means it, because, try as I might, he's getting to me. It's simple acts here and there that tell me he's more serious than I give him credit for. And not once has he given up. In fact, he presses hard without forcing me. I've never had a guy fight for me. It doesn't help that I also find him insanely attractive. If those women by the bathroom are anything to go by, I know I'm not the only one, and that thought frightens me a little.

The previews are already playing as we fully enter the theater and turn toward the stairs. Reid drops his arm as I follow Ivy and Dustin up the stairs, but they turn toward the middle rows, and I hesitate. Do I really want to sit next to them when I know for a fact that they're going to make out for half the movie? I mean, this was supposed to be a girls' thing, but…

"Let's go up top," Reid suggests quietly.

I bite the inside of my cheek. Sit next to a making-out couple, or sit next to the hottest guy I know? He makes that choice for me, gently nudging me to climb the steps. I go to the very top row where no one is sitting and slide into the aisle. Once I pick a seat, Reid sits next to me.

We settle in silence and take in the previews, but I'm not paying attention because the shared armrest? We're sharing it. Do I move my arm? Do I ask him to? My heart beats rapidly when his pinky brushes my finger. Was that deliberate? Or was it a twitch?

As the movie begins to play, he does it again, and my lips part. I sneak a glance at him, and that's when he smiles and gently moves his hand over, curling his fingers between mine. He slowly looks over at me. "Is this okay?" he asks after a moment.

I clear my throat, look at our joined hands, and nod. I might have a heart attack, but his holding my hand is something I simply cannot refuse. Because…I want it. I want that connection. I want to, just for a moment, pretend like I don't have a million walls. For a moment, I just want to be the girl I used to be, one who'd never been hurt so badly that she can't give easily the sweetest guy in the world a chance.

For a moment, I want to pretend. So I curl my fingers around his knuckles.

My phone buzzes in my pocket, so I pull it out with my free hand and look at the text.

Ivy
Oh my god! Oh my god! Tell me I don't need to rescue you!

I look up and see Ivy staring at us from her seat and blush so hard that my cheeks feel like they're on fire. Reid looks at the screen and chuckles under his breath. With the hand that's not holding mine, he holds out his hand and I don't know why, but I pass over the phone. He snaps a picture of our joined hands and sends it off to Ivy.

I watch as her face lights up when she gets the picture, hiding the screen from Dustin. She holds the phone to her chest and looks at me, little hearts practically dancing in her eyes.

Reid chuckles again, and I turn my attention back to him. He's doing something on my phone, and I frown as he gets into my contacts. He starts typing something into it, and when he's finished, he passes me back the phone.

I quickly look at what he did. He put his number into my phone.

Shocked, I glance up at him.

"No pressure," he says, his voice barely above the movie. "But it's there when or if you ever need it."

My breathing shallows as he looks at my parted lips. With Neil, he always pressured me to do things, but the way that Reid is going about it…I don't feel pressured whatsoever. In fact, all I have are these intense butterflies that damn near demand that I kiss him. And the way he's looking at my lips tells me he wants me to.

"You're really taking this off-limits thing to a whole new level," I whisper.

He flashes me a grin but never looks away from my lips. "I live on the edge."

"Always?"

He shakes his head and slides his gaze back up to mine. "Only with you."

My heart skips a beat. "Is it because you can afford to?" I ask, wanting an honest answer and knowing that he'll know what I mean by it.

He blinks, and I know he caught on to my meaning. "Where'd that come from?" he asks with a squeeze of my hand.

I shrug. "I was told you had a lot of money. I just want to make sure you're not hiding behind it."

Slowly, he nods. "My parents have the money. I only get an allowance for food, gas, and rent until I'm finished with college. Nothing more."

"And the nice car?"

"I got that when I turned sixteen."

My eyebrows rise. "It's rare for a teen not to crash their first car."

He shrugs and squeezes my hand again. "Like I said, I only live on the edge when I'm with you."

"Why?"

He reaches and touches my chin, and it's then that I realize how close we are. "Because you're worth every secret."

I glance at his lips and then back up at his eyes. "I'm glad that your parents aren't throwing money at you."

"I'm glad that my parents' money isn't all you see."

I shrug. "Money means nothing to me."

"Oh yeah? What does?"

I smile a little. "Wouldn't you like to know?"

He chuckles. "So you have secrets of your own. I get

it." He releases my chin and settles his hand on his lap. "So I heard you had college paid for. Did your parents-"

I shake my head. "It was all my own money."

"Care to share?"

Blushing, I shake my head. He doesn't need to know that I stripped to a bikini and posed for a million horny men, especially when I no longer look that way.

"More secrets." His eyes are intently back on my lips again.

"I have many."

He closes the distance and presses his lips to mine. It's over too quickly, but it was enough to make my pulse hammer. "Share them with me, Avery. Date me."

I look down at our joined hands. His fingers curl tightly around mine. "I can't," I whisper.

I'm surprised that he heard me, but he answers, "Why?"

"I'm not ready."

It takes a moment, but he brings my face back to his. "What did he do to you?"

I shake my head as a tear gathers in my eyes. It spills over, and he wipes it away.

"If I could go back in time, if I could turn back the time, I'd find your brother sooner so that I could find you. Then I'd have you, and you'd never have to go through the heartache your ex put you through. You wouldn't be in pieces with me trying to put you back together. It's a task I'm willing to take on, but I could have stopped it from ever happening to you. *That* is how much you mean to me, Avery."

"Yeah?" I ask with a sniffle.

He nods. "Your brother's *forbid me not* and everything."

I chuckle under my breath, and he smiles a little. "There's my girl," he adds.

"Your girl?"

He nods again, the smile never leaving his face. "If I have anything to say about it, you're off the market."

I don't tell him how the sound of that makes me want to kiss him and kiss him hard. I don't tell him that no one has talked to me the way he is. In this moment, I feel cherished, and I just want to feel that feeling a little longer before the movie is over and our little bubble is burst, and we go back to reality where I can't let him in—because I know it'll happen. As soon as the lights come back on, the walls will resurrect.

So instead, I rest my head against his shoulder, and he plants his lips on top of my hair, periodically kissing there throughout the rest of the movie.

And I can't help but think…I like the way he helps me escape. How it feels to be here, right now, pretending. How it feels to pretend that Neil never existed and that this is exactly where I was always meant to be.

CHAPTER 16
REID RATHE

I CAN'T PAY attention to the movie. She's curled against me, chuckling at the funny moments and snuggling in deeper during the cute ones. I continue to hold on to her hand because I know that I'm lucky to do such a simple act. But slowly—and I know this with certainty—she's getting used to me. She's thinking about letting me in. She's thinking about *us*.

A part of me wonders how much her ex did to her. I get the feeling it's worse than what Dustin has portrayed. What girl wouldn't give in by now? He had to have damaged her, maybe beyond repair. Maybe a piece of her that he took is something I'll never have. It kills me to know that, and if I could, I really would turn back time because we deserve to share all of our pieces. Together.

I just have to reassure her that I'll take any pieces she has left.

The movie comes to an end, and the lights come back on. I clench my jaw when she lets go of my hand, but I know we can't be caught holding them. She stretches and gathers herself to her feet. I follow and watch as she pulls at her fingers. "Thanks for letting me use you as a pillow."

"It was more than that, and you know it."

She ignores me and tries to fix her hair. "Is it sticking up in all the wrong places?"

I pinch a strand and tuck it behind her ear. "You look perfect, Avery."

I can feel her closing off again, and I start to panic. I can't show my panic though because it'll just make her close off even more, so instead, I let her walk past me and down the stairs to meet Dustin and Ivy.

We throw away our trash in the can inside the theater, and Ivy turns to us, creating a little circle just inside the dim hallway. "I really have to pee. Can I meet you guys in the lobby?"

Avery nods at the same time Dustin says, "I'll walk you there."

"I can walk myself," she harrumphs.

"Not at this time of night, you're not."

"He's right, Ivy. You should let him go with," Avery chimes in. Hell, if it was Avery needing to go to the bathroom, I'd follow her too. We live in a big city. Anything can happen, and knowing that it could riddles me with fear. I can only imagine Dustin has the same fear when it comes to protecting his girl.

She wrinkles her nose at him and says, "Fine."

They push through the door and disappear, leaving me with Avery. She blows out a breath and turns to me, opening her mouth to say something, and that's when I advance on her. I grab her around the waist and yank her to me. My lips crash down on hers, and at first, she stiffens, but it takes less than a second for her to melt against my chest and kiss me back.

The world fades away, and I kiss her with everything

I have. Everything I've been trying to tell her put into action. I can't stand that she's pulling away, and knowing that, when we step out that door, we go back to being a secret and me trying to convince her that I might be worth it anyway. That *we* would be worth it.

I slide a hand into her hair and angle her head so I can kiss her deeper. She moans into my mouth when I let my tongue slide against hers. She tastes like her with a hint of sweet soda.

With my chest pressed to hers, I can feel how fast her heart is beating. How much I affect her. How what we share is something more than just attraction.

The door opens, and Avery breaks the kiss to look and see who entered. Ivy stands there, a look of shock on her face. "Um. I just forgot my cell in my seat."

"We weren't doing anything," Avery quickly says.

"Bull." Ivy smiles slyly. "But you should probably stop because, if we don't get out there, Dustin will come looking for us and wonder why you two are standing in a dark hallway with kiss-swollen lips."

Ivy walks past us in search of her phone, and we stand there, staring at one another. I can't stand the silence, the words left unsaid. I break it. "You may be imperfect in your eyes, but you're perfect in mine. I'm begging you to let me in, Avery. Flaws. Walls. Pain. I want it all. Don't walk out those doors pretending that we didn't make some progress. Don't let me go. Don't shove me out. Don't close me off."

Her bottom lip wobbles. "I like you, Reid."

"I like you too."

She looks at the door. "Just give me time to learn how to trust again."

I close the distance, cup her cheek, and press a soft kiss to her eyebrow. "Luckily, I have all the time in the world."

And then I leave her waiting for Ivy while I head out of the theater and toward the lobby. I blow out an unsteady breath, hoping like hell she meant what she said.

CHAPTER 17
AVERY MOORE

"I'M GOING TO WORK. Do you need anything?" Ivy asks, popping into my doorway. "I can stop somewhere on the way back."

She's pulling her hair into a tight bun, the bun she always wears when she works at the diner, claiming it keeps it from dipping into unwanted syrup. It makes her face look sharper, too, but I've noticed that Dustin likes it when her hair is down. He always toys with it when he's over.

I've often fantasized about what it would be like to have Reid play with my hair that way.

I haven't seen or heard from Reid since last night, which is fine. Sort of. I miss him. I miss the way his hand held mine, the way he kissed me, and the way he spoke to me. And I was right about the walls returning once I stepped out of that theater and back into reality. However, they're not as strong as they once were.

"No," I say, looking back at my notebook.

"Not even a midnight snack?" She does that single eyebrow raise again, and again, I wonder how the hell she does that.

I shake my head. When Reid grabbed onto my waist last night, I was keenly aware of my weight. Neil would have never held me like that at this size. Hell, Neil never kissed me like that either, but that doesn't mean I don't still have insecurities just because Reid appears to be different.

"Not even a milkshake?"

I laugh and shake my head. "I'll be fine, but thanks though."

She eyes me skeptically, and I try not to shrivel under her gaze. I always ask for a snack, so she's probably wondering why tonight is different. "If you're sure."

"I am," I say firmly, picking up my textbook again.

"Okay." She shrugs and then points at me. "You look adorable by the way."

I look down at my too-big shirt and loose pajama shorts with flowers printed all over them. I'm not wearing a bra or underwear either, but she doesn't need to know that.

With an amused expression, I look back up at her. "I tried so hard for this look," I say sarcastically. "I'm glad my hard work paid off."

She shrugs. "You just look more relaxed than you have in a long time. Is this…does this have anything to do with the kiss I saw last night?"

"Nope," I lie.

"You're such a terrible liar," she says, laughing. "I'm glad to see the old you coming back."

"Thanks?"

"You're welcome. Okay," she breathes. She straightens her skirt. "I'm off. I'll catch you tomorrow if you're not up when I get back."

I nod and then wave her off, diving deep into the Spanish assignment due the day after tomorrow. I get lost in the work, going over Ivy's and my notes and the highlighted words in the textbook. At some point, I turn on the music to a low volume, and before I can sit back on my bed, a knock sounds at the door.

Frowning, I head out of my room and to the door. I pull it open, thinking it's Ivy, who has forgotten her keys, but instead, I find Reid standing there, looking nervously back at Dustin's door.

He's holding purple roses in one hand and his backpack in the other. "Reid?" I hiss, nervous that my brother will find us. Literally, all he has to do is open the door to find us. "What are you doing here?"

He cringes. "Can I come in?"

I step aside and let him in, softly shutting the door behind him. His massive frame feels like it takes up most of the apartment, and his delicious scent curls around the space in a matter of seconds.

"What's going on?" I ask.

He smiles when he turns to look at me. I glance at the flowers when he holds them out for me. "I brought you flowers."

My heart warms. "What for?"

"Because I like you." He shrugs. "And I have to butter you up."

I take the flowers from him and push my nose against the petals, inhaling. He remembered my favorite flower, and the notion doesn't go unnoticed. "Butter me up for…?"

He holds up his backpack while glowering. "Homework."

I laugh a little and set the flowers on the table. "Let me guess: Your notes are as crappy as mine."

Grimacing, he admits, "Guilty."

Sighing, I pinch the bridge of my nose. "This is why our little conversations in class shouldn't be happening." I say it, but I don't mean it. In fact, I find myself looking forward to the next Spanish class so that we can find out more about each other.

All he does is shrug. "Help me?"

"Well, you're in luck, actually. I was just working on the assignment."

His face lights up. "Really? What would you say about doing it together?"

I twist my lips to the side, contemplating. Being in my bedroom with him again will be torture because I remember literally everything about the last time we were in there.

He sees my hesitation. "Please?" he begs.

Defeated, knowing I can't resist him, I wave him toward my room. He follows me down the hall, and once he's inside my bedroom, he has a look around. "It looks different in the light."

His eyes land on the bed, and I blush because I know he's remembering what happened there.

"Um," I begin, pushing a hand through my hair. I travel over to the bed and make room for him. "You can sit here."

He opens his backpack and pulls out his textbook, notes, and supplies. Instead of sitting, he crawls onto my bed and lies down on his stomach, propping the book on my pillow. I can't help but zero in on his ass. It's perfectly round, and the muscles ripple as he shifts his legs around, getting comfortable.

Once he's set up, he looks back at me. "Coming?"

"This is a bad idea," I admit.

He laughs and pats the spot beside him. "We can keep our hands to ourselves."

Yeah. Maybe you can. But I'll be thinking about it the entire time.

Waving me over, he pulls out his notes, glances over, and sees Ivy's notes. He picks those up as I climb onto the bed with my stomach twisting into knots. Hell, I'm not even wearing a bra, and he hasn't commented on it, so maybe he will keep his hands to himself. Do I even want that? Damn my body for betraying me.

"These are amazing notes," he murmurs.

"Yeah, Ivy was nice enough to give them to me."

He glances over at me, and his eyes fall to my chest. I follow his gaze down and find my nipples pebbled. *Shit.*

"Eyes up here," I whisper.

He flicks his gaze to mine, and for a moment, I find heat in them before he shakes his head. "Sorry. They're just...sorry."

"Men and boobs," I tease, rolling my eyes.

He laughs. "I'm a guy. I notice these things, especially on a hot girl."

"Ah, so you look at half of the female population's boobs."

"Nope," he says, popping the 'p' and going back to the notes. "Just yours."

I stare at the side of his face for a little too long because he looks back at me and shakes the notes. "Eyes on the homework, Avery."

"Right." I clear my throat and pick up my textbook. I reread a paragraph three times before my eyes start roaming his backside. His shirt is tight enough to reveal the muscles in his back, and they flex every time he leafs through the notes.

Every part of my body thrums right now, and I squirm as a need arises between my legs.

"You can touch, you know," he whispers while he jots down some notes on his laptop.

"Touch what?" I whisper back.

"Me."

"That would be distracting."

He looks over at me, and we stare at each other for a while. "You're already distracted," he points out huskily.

I wet my bottom lip as he flips over, homework forgotten, and rests his hands behind his head. My eyes skate along his body, all the way down to the erection pressing against his jeans.

I gulp.

"How about this? You get to touch me until it gets too heated."

"I don't know…"

"Touch me, Avery."

I flick my gaze back to his and find that the heat has returned and that he's completely serious. Being braver than I feel, I reach and slip my hand under his shirt. His skin ripples as my fingers trace over his abs, but he holds still, letting me explore.

When my hand travels higher, he lifts himself slightly off the bed and takes off his shirt. Saliva pools in my mouth as his abs contract until he lies back down. His body is that of a god and my mouth salivates at the sight of him.

"Stop," he whispers.

"Your turn?"

He nods and props himself up on an elbow. He reaches and brushes his finger against my ankle. Slowly, his hand travels up my calf as I count my breaths to keep them even. His fingers leave a burning sensation as they travel, and when he starts touching my inner thigh, my breathing quickens despite my efforts. He skates his hand by my shorts, toying with the hem of them.

"Stop," I hiss out.

"Again?"

I nod, and he lies back down. I press my hand to his forearm, skating it up his arm and leisurely over his shoulder. His skin is like butter, smooth and silky. I let my fingers trail over his collarbone, and his eyes flutter when I travel between his pecks. My hand goes lower, dipping between each ab, and when I reach his belly button, I circle it. His stomach hollows out and then flexes. I'm mesmerized by the way his body responds, and I push them even lower, toying with the waistband of his jeans.

His cock jumps when I slip them under and run my fingers from hip bone to hip bone.

Through gritted teeth, he says, "Stop."

We're both breathing hard at this point, our inhales and exhales in time with each other. He props himself back on his elbow and reaches once more. His hand goes for the waistband of my shorts and slips up my shirt.

I freeze.

His eyes flick to mine, and he stops his advance. He must sense my rising panic because he murmurs, "I happen to like your curves, Avery. Relax for me."

I take a deep breath, and on my exhale, he begins moving again. Without seeing where he's going, because my shirt is in the way, his calloused palm moves along my stomach. I begin to relax while studying his face because all that's there is lust. Attraction. Want.

His hand doesn't tremble as it goes higher and brushes against the bottom of my breasts. I moan and arch into his touch, and he raises his hand higher and cups one of them. I arch into him and regretfully say, "Stop."

He groans and hangs his head while removing his hand.

"My turn. Take off your pants, please."

He raises his eyebrows but does as I ask, unbuttoning his jeans and sliding them down his legs. "It's not fair that I'm almost naked and you're still fully clothed."

I shush him, and his lips seal shut as I climb on top of him and hover just above his erection. His head rests against the pillow as his hands go to my hips. "Ready?" I ask.

"For?" he says through clenched teeth.

I giggle, enjoying this game way too much. "Keeping time. I get only twenty seconds. Don't let me go over."

"Right." He clears his throat. "Ready."

Lowering myself onto him, I search for release against the throbbing between my legs and grind my clit against his cock. The fabric between is a little cumbersome, but honestly, it adds to the feel. It'd feel better if there were none, I know that, but I'll take what I can get.

His fingers tighten their grip on my hips, and he curses under his breath. I make another pass of my hips and tip my head back at the delicious feel of the pressure. It makes my stomach tighten and my pussy clench. I begin rotating my hips, our breathing and the music playing softly in the background.

At this point, he's helping me rotate my hips back and forth. I can feel myself so close to release. My abdomen tightens, and fire lights up in my veins as a slight sweat breaks out along my spine.

"Time?" I whisper.

"Fuck the time," he growls and flips me over.

"What are you doing?" I ask breathlessly. No one has handled me that way. Especially with my weight.

"What we both want," he says, snagging the waistband of my shorts and slowly pulling them down my legs. He drops them on top of my laptop. Next, he slips out of his boxer briefs and lifts one of my legs to wrap around his hip.

Scattered among notes and textbooks, he pushes inside.

We moan together, and my walls ripple around him. He waits there, letting me adjust, before he takes my mouth in a searing kiss. Our tongues immediately tangle, and he starts moving inside me. He's gentle, both in his kiss and his movements. Just like whatever is going on between us, my climax builds in a slow burn.

I moan into his mouth when he hikes my leg higher and goes even deeper. His fingers tighten around my thigh while the other rests by my head.

"So beautiful," he says when my moans turn deeper, my climax building to an all-time high. "So stunning."

He trails kisses down my jaw and to my ear where he nibbles on the lobe and whispers, "Absolutely breathtaking."

And this time, I believe him. He's said it before, but in this moment, in the heat of passion, I know he means it. This isn't just a fuck, a quick release; this means something. It's deliberate.

A portion of my walls cracks and fractures away as I grip his back and dig my nails into his skin, holding onto him, onto this moment.

With my shirt riding up at our motion, his stomach touches mine, and it's the most delicious feeling in the world. It's completely comforting to feel his skin on mine.

My climax builds and builds, and then I shatter around him. He pumps his hips faster, riding out my climax as I groan his name until he pulls out and comes all over my stomach with a deep moan.

When he's finished, and our breathing is slowly coming down from a ragged pace, he flicks his gaze to mine before climbing off of me, bending over the bed, and angling my head to kiss me passionately.

"Towel?" he asks.

"Bathroom," I say, pointing.

He slides his underwear back on and exits my room, heading to the bathroom. He's back in no time with a wet washcloth, and he cleans up my stomach with a gentle touch. When he's done, he tosses it in the hamper.

"This is not why I came over, I swear." The guilt on his face makes me smile. He's gripping the back of his neck and I can tell he's about to start pacing.

"I know."

"You do?"

I nod. I sit up and pick up my shorts, slipping them on. "I fully believe you came here for homework."

"So you're not mad?"

"No."

He drops his hand and breathes a sigh of relief. "Okay, good." He flicks his gaze to the floor then back to me. "What does this mean?"

I twitch my lips to the side. "I don't know. I know it means something, but I'm…I'm so jumbled, Reid."

"Okay." He slowly nods. "So we don't label it. It happened, we enjoyed it, and…maybe it'll happen again?"

I know the meaning behind his question. He enjoyed the connection just as much as I did. I give him a small smile and say, "I'd like that."

A grin spreads across his face, and then he looks around the floor for his jeans. He picks them up and puts them on. "Homework?"

I laugh and scoot over to my side. "Probably should."

He settles in next to me, grips my chin, and presses a kiss to my lips. And then he gets to work, and I can't help but stare at him a little longer. I know he's trying not to make a big deal about it, afraid to scare me off, but I can't help but wonder what it would be like to have him and call him mine.

CHAPTER 18
AVERY MOORE

"WHO ARE YOU TEXTING SO MUCH?" I ask Ivy. We're on our way back from the college, ready to climb into pajamas and eat pizza until we're so stuffed we'll have to find someone to roll us to our bedrooms.

There's an extra pep in my step, and though I haven't heard from Reid in a few days, I'm still on the high of our...encounter. The way he made me feel. The things he said to me.

The more I think about it, the more I'm warming up to the idea of him, but there's one problem. My brother said no to Reid at the beginning of all this, and when he finds out—because he will—it'll be the ultimate betrayal from me all over again. I don't know if I could go through him not talking to me for...forever. I would be breaking his rule even though that rule wasn't given to me. Even if my brother doesn't end up blaming me and not talking to me ever again, he'll do it to Reid. The thought of those two not being friends anymore...I just can't wrap my head around it.

That thought alone is something I have to consider. I may have warmed up to Reid, may have fantasized about what it would be like to have him, but would I really ask him—us—to give up our relationship with Dustin just to have one ourselves?

"Your brother," Ivy says. There's a look of concentration on her face, and red flags rise.

"Are you two fighting?"

She twists her lips to the side, but her fingers continue to tap on her screen. It's amazing that she can even walk like this. I'd have tripped and fallen by now. "More like bickering."

"Over what?" I've seen them bicker, but I can tell whatever they're talking about is sapping her energy.

"Nothing," she says, pocketing her phone with a grimace.

"Sure doesn't look like nothing," I grumble.

"So," she says, pushing hair from her face that the wind whipped there and tightening her backpack straps. "Have you texted Reid yet?"

Biting my bottom lip is my only answer. I told her about what happened in my bedroom the other night. How could I not? It was a pivotal moment in…whatever we are. I needed someone to process this with.

Ivy had sat and listened like the good friend she is. Even coming home exhausted from the diner, she sat there with me while I spilled the entire situation. At the end of it, she had a smile on her face and gave me a big hug. I don't think she realizes how much trouble *she* could get into if Dustin found out she knew too.

"Oh, come on, Avery. Give the poor man a break, and let him save your number to his phone."

I shake my head. "Honestly, I like it like this."

"The old-fashioned way of courting?"

A smile spreads my cheeks. "Yeah, when you put it like that. It's more fun."

"You're just making him work for it."

"And enjoying it," I admit quietly.

"Torture," she murmurs. "The poor guy."

I laugh. "Oh, come on. You're even getting entertainment out of this."

She cringes and then chuckles. "Guilty."

Bumping shoulders with her, we cross the crosswalk and head toward our apartment building. "Are you sure you don't want to talk about what's going on between you and Dustin?"

Her mood sours a little. "Oh, you'll find out soon enough."

I frown at her. "What do you mean?"

"He told me it wasn't a big deal. But honestly, I'm freaking out and therefore know you're going to freak out."

Sighing, we round the building and into the parking lot. "What did my brother do now?"

"Well…" She puckers her lips. "Both him and Reid."

"Just spit it out, girl. Stop dancing around the problem."

She glances at me then looks forward and points. I follow her line of sight, and a scowl takes over my face.

There are a few trucks with furniture in the back, and people are unloading it. Nice furniture, by the looks of it. Upon a squint, they're people I recognize from Dustin's party when I first moved here.

"Who the hell is moving into the building midsemester?"

She snatches my wrist as we pick up our pace a little bit, causing a sinking feeling in the pit of my stomach. "He said it wasn't a big deal, but I can see that you're getting mad, and I'm starting to panic."

"No…no, he wouldn't," I whisper angrily as it begins to click in my head.

"Oh, but he did," she grumbles, letting my wrist go as we approach the trucks. Just as we reach them, Dustin and Reid come out of the building, intent on grabbing more furniture to take upstairs to Dustin's apartment. *Their* apartment.

Anger simmers in the pit of my gut. It takes everything I have not to march up to Reid and demand to know what the hell he was thinking.

The boys turn to us and smile, but their smiles fade when they see our expressions. I've never been good at hiding my feelings.

"What's going on?" I ask, trying to keep the rage from my tone. I probably failed, but whatever. I'm beyond caring.

Dustin slaps a hand down on Reid's bare shoulder. They're both dressed similarly in a cutoff shirt and a pair of gym shorts, and if I didn't know any better, I'd say that they came straight from working out. "Reid is moving in."

"What about your other roommate?"

"He moved out yesterday," Dustin answers, frowning. "Why are you so upset?"

I glance at Reid, who is trying to hide the smile on his face. "Don't you have your own apartment?"

He shrugs. "I gave it up."

"To slum it in college apartments?"

He shrugs again and then smirks the sexiest smirk there ever was. But it's not going to work on me. I stare him down.

"His parents have cameras on his apartment. It's why he doesn't have any parties and is always here," Dustin divulges.

"What? Why?" I ask.

"They own the building," Reid answers.

"So, he's breaking free," Dustin says, puffing his chest like he had everything to do with Reid's newfound freedom.

Someone calls Dustin over to the furthest truck, leaving me, Ivy, and Reid standing there on the sidewalk. I simmer with so much anger that I'm sure my face is beet red.

"Why are you so mad?" he asks quietly.

"Oh, I don't know," Ivy says sarcastically. "Maybe because you're playing a dangerous game."

He crosses his arms. "How so?"

I poke his chest, and my finger bounces off hard muscle. "How the hell are we supposed to keep this from Dustin when you literally live in the same apartment as him?"

A smile grows on his face. "So there is something between us?"

I throw my hands up in the air. "I thought the other night solidified that."

He raises his eyebrows. "So we're dating?"

"What? No."

"So we're seeing other people?"

"No!"

He rubs at his forehead. "I'm so confused."

"You and me both," Ivy says, touching his shoulder as she passes him. "I'm going inside while you two figure this out." She pauses and whispers over her shoulder, "But you might want to keep your voices down."

She heads inside, and Reid turns back to me. "What are we, Avery?"

I shuffle my weight from one foot to the other. "I don't know. Okay? I haven't figured that out yet."

"Why?"

"Because! Have you not thought about the consequences?"

He glances over at Dustin, who's laughing at something one of his buddies said. "I have."

"Then surely you know this isn't a good idea. And an even worse idea now that you live across the hall."

He looks back at me, studies my face, takes me in, and I try not to squirm. "You're worth it."

I look down at my feet, the desire to say it back on the tip of my tongue. "You've made this so much harder," I murmur.

"He's going to find out eventually," he whispers back. "We should just tell him."

I whip my gaze back up to his, panic making my eyes wide. "No!" I hiss.

"Why not?"

"Because you'll lose him as a friend, and I'll lose him too. And even Ivy's relationship could be in jeopardy."

He slides a hand over his mouth and drops it to his side. "Not if we're honest. You can't know for certain how he'll react."

I shake my head. "But I do."

"How?"

My chest heaves as I inhale slowly and push it out. He patiently waits for me to explain. "When we were younger, Dustin had this dog. He was so sweet, a great dog, but he liked to run out the door and push his way through gates. One time, I was playing with the dog outside, wasn't paying attention when I went through the gate, and he pushed through." I swallow thickly as the memory surfaces. The sound of the brakes. The blare of the horn. The pitch of the yelp. "He was hit by a car. We put him down that very night because the damage was beyond repair. It took Dustin forever to talk to me after that night. To acknowledge that I existed. I won't…I won't lose my brother again. I won't betray him again."

He reaches for me, thinks better of it, and flexes his

hand as he settles it at his side again. "This is different, Avery. This isn't death. This is happiness. Surely your brother wants you to be happy."

I push a hand through my hair, fighting back tears. "I just…we can't label this right now, Reid. I have to figure this out first."

"We can figure it out together."

I look back up into his eyes and see the sincerity in them. We stand there for a while, simply having a silent conversation about where we go from here and if we do it together or alone.

"I have feelings for you," he eventually whispers.

Swallowing thickly, I nod. "I know."

"Do you have feelings for me?"

I look over at Dustin, who catches my gaze and gives me a little wave. I wave back as I say, "I do."

"Then we got this," he murmurs when I turn my attention back to him. "We don't have to label anything. I'm content simply being in your space."

"Me too," I whisper.

He looks around to make sure no one is watching before he closes the space between us and kisses my forehead. "We'll continue this conversation some other time." He steps away as I nod. "If we continue to talk, your brother will start to—"

"Figure it out, I know, I know." I exhale sharply. "Okay. So move in, and we'll just tread carefully while we figure this all out."

He nods, dares a touch to my chin, and jogs toward Dustin. I watch as Dustin turns around at the sound of Reid's footfalls and slaps him on the back as they climb into the back of the pickup.

This won't end well, whatever this is between us. I know it won't. I know my brother. The question is: How much am I willing to risk?

With a bit of nausea at the prospect, I head inside. I have every intention of taking Ivy out for a drink. I need a detox, and alcohol will have to be the antidote tonight.

CHAPTER 19
REID RATHE

IT'S WELL PAST MIDNIGHT, and I'm *still* unpacking. I didn't think I had this much stuff, but I guess I was wrong.

I hang a shirt in the closet and turn to the pile laid out on my unmade bed. I'm bone tired, but with the weekend starting tomorrow, I promise myself a nap at some point.

Instead of grabbing the next shirt, I sit next to the pile and rake a hand down my tired face. My mind wanders to the conversation that Avery and I had earlier today. She was upset, and though it was cute, she had valid concerns. For me, however, it's black and white. I want her, she wants me, so we should make it happen. She sees everything in color. It's not simple for her.

At least, she doesn't want us to see other people. Not that I would. She's all I want, and I have tunnel vision when it comes to her. But it's comforting to know that I'm the only guy in her life. We may not be dating, but we're as close as we're going to get…for now. I have every intention of changing that because, clearly, what I'm doing is working.

My phone beeps, and I dig it out of my pocket, wondering who the hell would be texting me so late.

I open the phone and click on the text app.

Ivy sent a picture, and I bring the phone close to my face to make it all out. It's a picture of Avery. She's laughing with a drink in her hand as they sit on the stool of some bar they're at.

A follow-up text comes next.

Ivy
We may need a ride. Our last Uber driver was creepy.

I curse under my breath.

How drunk is she?

Ivy
Plastered. She's going to feel it tomorrow.

Me
And you?

Ivy
Not as bad as her.

Me
Do you want me to bring Dustin?

Ivy
No! She's going on and on about you. Dustin can't hear it.

I roll my neck.

Which bar are you at?

She rattles off an address, and I stand up and pocket my phone. Is she really so stressed that she needed to get drunk? The last time I saw her drunk was at Dustin's party, and she looked like she was trying to escape then.

My guts twist inside me as I pluck up my car keys and quietly sneak out of the apartment.

As I pull up to the bar, I take in the surroundings. The bar is a hole in the wall, a real fixer-upper, and there's a whole host of people smoking outside. I can smell the cigarette smoke from here.

I note that none of them are our age, which isn't surprising, considering the bar is downtown. How did they find this place? Did they play Eenie Meenie Miney Mo in a Google search? However they found it, it probably had everything to do with the acceptance of fake IDs. All my friends have them, including myself, so it's not surprising that Avery and Ivy have some.

I climb out of my car and hold my breath as I weed through the puffs of cigarette smoke. As soon as I'm inside, I scan my surroundings. For a weeknight, there are a lot of people here. The place smells like grease and beer, and there's a slight stench of body odor.

On my scan of the room, my eyes land on Ivy, who is emerging from the bathroom. I head to her immediately, and she smiles once she spots me.

"You made it!"

"You're drunk," I state as she sways. Heels probably weren't the best idea if she had planned on getting drunk tonight. I catch her by the arm before she has a chance to fall over.

"A little drunker than when I texted you, yes. What are you? My dad?"

I chuckle under my breath. "No, but Dustin would kill me if you got hurt and I did nothing to prevent it. Like, ask you to take off the damn heels."

"Ew, I'm not putting my feet on this floor." Her nose wrinkles in disgust. She leans in closer to me and whispers, "Does Dustin know you're here?"

I shake my head. "His room was dark when I left. He's asleep."

She straightens. "Good. He doesn't need to see his sister like this."

"Speaking of, where is she?"

She turns me around and points to the bar. It takes me a moment, but I see the back of her head among the sea of people. She's definitely drunk, and she's talking to the people on her right. They laugh at something she says, and a smile crosses my face.

Ivy chuckles under her breath. "She's been making friends."

"I see that."

"You should have heard her talk about you."

I look over at her. "What do you mean?"

"Dude, she has it bad," Ivy says, waving her hand around. Because she's intoxicated, the movement is practically in slow motion.

"For?"

She pokes me in the arm. "You! She won't stop talking about you."

A smile spreads across my face. "Bad or good things?"

"A mix of both. Is your favorite flower really a dandelion?"

I laugh under my breath as my response.

"You know that's a weed, right?"

I shrug and start to make my way over to her, but Ivy grabs my arm. I frown down at her.

"Sorry, but, uh…don't be mad at her. I encouraged her to get drunk so she'd spill everything that's on her mind."

Shaking my head, I say, "I'm not mad at her. She's an adult, and if getting drunk helps her solve her problems, then so be it."

She lets go of my arm, grinning from ear to ear. "You really are a good guy, Reid."

"Thanks," I murmur before heading to Avery. I want to get to my girl. I *need* to get to her.

When I reach her, I press my stomach into her back. She stops whatever she was saying to her stool neighbor and looks up at me, her head bumping into my chest. "Oh shit," she says.

I chuckle, bend down, and kiss her on the lips upside down. "Is that how we're greeting me now?"

"You must be the boyfriend," the lady next to her says. I look over at her and take in her red hair pinned back by a bandana and the fringe of her biker outfit.

Avery frowns and looks at the woman. "I told you, Brenda. He's not my boyfriend."

Brenda points at her. "You need to make it official."

"You think?" she asks, leaning back into me. I hold up her weight by keeping my feet planted on the ground so that I can be her support.

"Yeah," Brenda says before taking a swig of her beer. "When you talked about him, I didn't think he'd be such a hunk, but now that he's here, you need to snatch him before someone else does."

Avery curses under her breath. "I didn't think of that."

"I'm not going anywhere," I interject, but they don't listen to me.

"That's right," Brenda says, clinking her beer bottle against Avery's shot glass of what smells like tequila. "Screw the brother, and take your man."

"Oh, oh!" Ivy says beside me. "Tell him about what you'd do to Avery's ex!"

"Easy," Brenda huffs. She takes several more gulps of her beer before waving the bartender down and asking for another. "You fly to his place, knock on his door, and then shoot him in the balls when he answers."

I cringe at the thought, but Avery claps and looks up at me. "Do your parents have a plane?"

"No," I say, clearing my throat and trying like hell not to cup my own balls. "But even if they did, there'd be no family jewels assaults."

"But he so deserves it," Ivy hisses.

Brenda toasts Avery to it, and Avery downs her shot. Avery then holds out her shot glass to the bartender. "It doesn't burn like it used to."

I take the shot glass from her and stare the bartender down. He holds up his hands and walks down the way to fill someone else's demands. "I think that's enough for tonight," I whisper in her ear.

Her bottom lip sticks out. "But Brenda, Ivy, and I are having so much fun."

I turn her on the stool and settle between her legs. I then tip her head up to mine and kiss her tequila-tasting lips. "You can have fun."

"Oh yeah?" There's hope in her eyes.

"Yes. In bed."

A smirk crosses her face. "With you?"

I laugh under my breath. "Not tonight. I won't take advantage of your state."

She twirls her finger in front of my face. "It wouldn't be taking advantage if I asked for it."

I press another kiss to her lips and help her off the

stool. She wobbles a little bit, but I have ahold of her arm. She giggles as I say, "Not happening, baby girl." I glance back at Ivy to make sure she's following us out the door.

"I'm coming, I'm coming," she says, her shoes in one hand and her cell phone in the other.

I guide the girls through the smoke and back to my car. Opening the passenger side, I help Avery inside and shut the door. Ivy climbs into the back seat, and I head to the driver's side, climb in, make sure everyone has their seatbelts on, and start the car.

They spend the entire time back giggling about their night and the friends they made, but me? My mind slips into what that Brenda lady said. Avery told her what happened with her ex. I'd be lying if I said it didn't sting that she hadn't told me yet. I want to know everything about Avery. The things that make her laugh. The tragedies that make her cry. And everything in between.

By the time we get home, Avery is passed out in the driver's seat, and Ivy is nearly there as well. I park the car and sit there for a minute, gazing at Avery and her soft sleeping sounds. I reach out and brush my knuckles down the side of her face, savoring the moment where, just for a minute, I pretend like she can tell me anything. Like there are no obstacles we have to hurdle and we can just be…normal. *Us.*

"Are we home?" Ivy asks sleepily in the back.

I nod. "Do you need help in?"

She shakes her head and starts to get out of the car. I exit as well and head to Avery's side. Once the door is open, Ivy asks, "Want me to wake her?"

I shake my head and scoop her up into my arms. Ivy shuts the door, and we head inside where she also opens every door for me. Avery remains completely unaware that she's being carried. She'd probably take issue with it if she did. I know she has issues with her weight, but it doesn't bother me one bit.

Once we're inside the apartment, I head to her room and lay her on the bed, head on the pillow. Next, I remove her shoes, set them aside, and kiss her on the forehead.

When I'm done, I head back out into the living room. Ivy is gulping down water in the kitchen, and I'm just about to leave, but I pause. She looks at me over her glass before she sets it down. "What?"

"Avery won't give me her number."

Her nose scrunches. "I know. She's enjoying it too much without that added bonus."

I purse my lips, trying to think of how to ask this. When no sly way comes to me, I ask, "You wouldn't be willing to give it to me, would you?"

I expect an immediate protest, but instead, her face brightens. She snatches her phone off the counter, and her fingers fly quickly across the screen. A few seconds later, my phone dings with an incoming text. I open it up to the shared contact and quickly save it to my phone before pocketing it.

"Thanks."

She waves me off. "She doesn't know what's good for her sometimes."

"I've noticed."

"You're changing her, you know."

I give her a small smile as my heart warms. "I know."

She crosses the kitchen and pats my arm. Before passing me and heading down the hall, she says, "Keep it up, Romeo."

"I'll try."

She whips around with surprise on her face. I don't have time to ask her what's wrong. Instead, she holds up a finger, telling me to wait. She dashes to her bedroom, and I don't have to wait long for her to reemerge. Heading to me, she holds out a calendar with a woman in a bikini.

I take it from her questioningly. "What do you want me to do with this?"

A mischievous grin takes over her face. "So you can keep track of the dates."

I look at the calendar's year. "This is from two years ago."

She nods like a bobblehead. "Good night, Reid."

Frowning, I watch her retreating back, wondering what the hell just happened. Instead of leaving the calendar behind, because I don't want to hurt her feelings, I take it with me back to my apartment.

CHAPTER 20
AVERY MOORE

THIS IS the worst hangover in the history of hangovers.

I groan as I flip over in my bed and stare at the ceiling. At the same time, a soft knock comes on my door. I don't bother answering, and it doesn't matter anyway because Ivy lets herself in.

Squinting at the hall light, I make a hissing sound.

"Oh good, you're up," Ivy croaks. "Did we do a lot of screaming last night? My throat is so hoarse."

I shake my head and then frown. "I don't know. It's all a little jumbled."

She steps into my room, and it's then that I see she's holding a Gatorade in one hand and a bottle of Tylenol in the other. Slowly, I sit up, making sounds of a grateful person as I greedily grab both items.

I pop two pills and down it with half the Gatorade bottle while she takes a seat at the edge of my bed.

"How did we get home?" I ask after my last swallow.

"Reid," she answers, pushing her messy hair out of her face.

My eyes go wide. "Dustin?"

She shakes her head and flops back onto my bed, her legs dangling off the edge. "He doesn't know."

"Thank God." I set the Gatorade beside me and rub the sleep from my eyes. My eyes swivel about the room and land on the mirror. My mouth drops open in horror. "Did I look like this last night?"

My hair looks worse than Ivy's, like I spent the day tangling it into knots, and my makeup is smeared across my face.

She giggles. "No. I have pictures to prove it too."

I breathe a sigh of relief and then climb off the bed. "I need a shower," I admit as I hobble to my closet, gather my clothes, and head to the bathroom. When I'm finished and my teeth are brushed, I comb through my hair as I head back into my room. Ivy is gone already, probably to Dustin's so he can spend the day nursing her hangover.

Sitting on my bed, I continue to get the knots out of my wet hair, and when my phone's text alert goes off, I head to my dresser where someone put it last night.

I set the brush down and pick up the phone. I frown and open it up. My heart stops dead in my chest at the picture of me in the bikini from two years ago…attached to Reid's text.

My heart skips a beat, and I swear for that split second that it's going to stop completely.

How the hell did you find that picture?

Him
Ivy.

Me
And I assume she gave you my number too?

Him
Yep.

Me
I'm going to kill her.

Him
Nah. She's just looking out for you.

Me
How is giving you that calendar looking out for me?

Him
Think about it.

I sit back on my bed with a harrumph. She knows I don't like that picture because it's of the girl I used to be. What I used to represent. The girl I no longer am and can't find. Well, I can. Every time I am with Reid, I feel a little of the girl return. And maybe that was the point of giving it to him, to show him who I was before Neil.

Him
Ah, yes. Understanding.

Me
I'm still going to be mad at her.

Him
Only for a little while, though.

Me
Maybe.

Him
You don't like this picture, do you?

My fingers hover over the keyboard as I think of what to say and how to say it.

I don't resemble that girl anymore. It's a reminder of what I'm not.

Him
I didn't know you then, but I like you better now. This girl looks lost.

I frown and scroll back up to stare at the picture. He's not wrong. There's a certain amount of ignorance in my expression like I couldn't believe what I was doing, that I was there and posing for a whole bunch of men.

And now?

Him
Weathered. Not lost.

I smile.

You make me sound old.

He sends a nodding GIF.

I like my women older.

A laugh bubbles out of my chest.

Aren't you just the smooth talker?

Him
You should know this by now.

Me
Joke's on me then.

Him
So I have a question, and you don't have to answer it if you don't want to.

I cringe, all the possibilities coming to light.

Okay...

Him
Is the modeling what gave you money for college?

I blow out a heavy breath.

Yes.

Him
Okay.

Me
That's it? No rage? No jealousy?

A knock sounds at my door, and I set down the phone to go answer it. As soon as I do, I find Reid standing there. I quickly let him in, about to reprimand him for possibly getting caught. Once he's inside, he turns to look at me. He comes to me immediately and kisses me, grabbing my jaw and tilting my head to deepen it.

I moan into his mouth as he backs me up into the door. God, why does he taste good all the damn time.

He breaks the kiss and rests his forehead against mine. "That was part of your past, Avery. I'll never judge you for your past. We all have one, and I know yours isn't pleasant. I just wish you'd share it with me instead of having your friends share pieces of it for you."

I glance away, my heart hammering in my chest. He rubs his thumb along my jaw as he waits for me to sort my thoughts.

"Tell me, Avery. Tell me what happened."

"With what?" I ask, feigning innocence.

He tilts my head back to his. "Tell me about what happened with your ex."

"I can't."

He searches my eyes. "You can."

"Why do you want to know so bad? If my past is my past, and we all have one, can't we just pretend it doesn't exist?"

He rests his forehead against mine again. "But your past is very present. It's stopping us from being *us.* Tell me; let me help you."

I clear my throat from the lump that's forming there. "Ivy and Dustin could walk in at any time."

He shakes his head. "He took her to the diner for pancakes. It's just you and me."

Tears gather in my eyes. "It's too painful."

"Then tell me what you can. Start from the beginning and tell me what you can about the rest."

The understanding in his voice is my undoing. Before I know it, the story is being told. "Neil and I met in high school. We were high school sweethearts, and he was kind and attractive to me at first, the nerdy girl and the jock. A dream come true, a fairy tale, right?"

He nods, encouraging me to continue.

"But that changed. I didn't realize it changed until it was too late and I had moved across the country to be with him and attend the same college. We didn't share a dorm because it wasn't allowed. Instead, I had a roommate, Vanessa, that I got really close to. Neil would come over and hang out with us, and looking back…I should have known…"

He brushes a tear from my cheek. "Should have known what?"

I swallow thickly. "One night, he proposed, which came as a huge surprise to me because we'd hardly been intimate for months. We started drifting apart, and I thought we were falling apart, but when he proposed, I thought it'd fix everything. Until I saw a used pregnancy test in Vanessa's drawer. I was happy for her...until I realized she wasn't dating anyone and hadn't gone out in weeks due to finals. Neil came over as I was questioning her with my suspicions, and I saw the look they shared. The baby was theirs. While I was in class, he was cheating on me."

He wipes away more tears and pulls me in close. "The worst part of it is Vanessa said I could have him still. That we could raise the baby as our own because she didn't want kids."

"I'm guessing you said no," he says into my hair.

I nod against him, sniffling. "I gave the ring back, and when I did, he...he...he called me fat. Boring. Said he'd never imagine himself being stuck with someone like me and how I wasn't what he signed up for."

He squeezes me and rocks me back and forth, and we're silent for a moment, me reliving my past and him digesting it. It was like it was yesterday for me, and saying it all out loud leaves me raw and vulnerable. But in his arms, I realize it doesn't hurt as much as it used to.

Eventually, he breaks the silence. "He should have never said things that aren't true."

"They aren't?"

He tips my chin until it's resting on his collarbone. Through my unshed tears, I see him give me a sad smile and shake his head. "I've seen what you used to look like and what you look like now. I mean it when I tell you how gorgeous you are. How stunning. I'd never lie to you, Avery, but he would. He *did* lie to you, in more ways than one."

"Yeah, I guess."

He presses a kiss to my lips. "No guessing. I'm right

this time. You once said that I reminded you of him. Is that still true?"

I think about it for a moment, blinking back the tears. Eventually, I come to a conclusion. "You're nothing like him."

"Good," he says right before he takes my mouth.

The kiss is passionate, heated, and filled with all the things the English language can't describe. I melt into him, my wet tears mixing with the kiss. My hands skirt under his shirt until I find skin and dig my nails in, holding on with everything I have.

He must understand that I need his skin because he breaks the kiss, takes off the shirt, and then takes off mine. They plop to the floor, and his lips find mine again as our skin meets in the middle. I can feel his erection through his sweatpants when he presses me against the door once more, holding me in place as he does what he wants to my mouth.

Our hands roam each other's bodies until he's had enough, lifts me up like I weigh nothing at all, and carries me to my bedroom. We remain glued to each other's lips until he lays me down on the bed, pulls my shorts down, and shucks his sweatpants.

Climbing onto the bed, he settles between my legs on his knees. His eyes roam my body, and I fight not to cover myself up, but the feeling is eased when he says, "So goddamn beautiful."

And then he settles on top of me and slides inside me with ease. We both groan as my walls stretch around him, sucking him in deeper. He starts to move inside me, balancing on one hand as the other skates over my body, his calloused palm touching every inch of my belly. When he reaches my breast, he goes over the mound before paying attention to my nipple and tweaking it.

I arch into the touch and whisper his name, wrapping

my legs tightly around his hips and encouraging him to pick up the pace. He listens, but his hand continues to explore my torso, the action saying more than words ever could.

In this moment, I don't feel like that fat girl. I don't feel like the boring girl. I feel seen, validated, and cherished. Wanted. Desired. And lastly, loved.

We haven't said the words yet, but I can feel myself falling for him. Hell, I already have. He's given me no reason not to. He's done everything right and then some. And I think…

As I stare up into his eyes, I think he feels the same, because the feeling in my heart is reflected in his gaze. This is deeper than, "I have feelings for you."

And the shocker of it all? I'm not scared of it.

My climax builds, and I start to whisper his name over and over again with every passing second. And then I explode, my pussy milking him. His breathing picks up pace as I ride out the waves, and soon, he's falling over the hill with me, pulling out and coming on my stomach like we've done in the past.

"Are you okay?" he asks.

I nod, and he climbs off of me in search of a washcloth. He returns and cleans me up, and once it's in the hamper, we get dressed.

"Still not dating?" he asks with humor in his tone.

I laugh back but sober quickly. When I say nothing, he looks up at me from buttoning his jeans. "Yes, we…we're dating."

His eyes widen in surprise, and he kneels before me. "You don't have to say that just because I asked. If you're not ready yet, I won't push it."

I shake my head. Everything he has done for me has led up to this moment. Every doubt I've had about him has been stripped bare and completely erased. I don't know how he did it - how he broke down my walls, but here I am, looking into his eyes and declaring, "I want to. I want *you.*"

He grins before gripping the back of my neck and kissing me. I indulge for a moment before I press my hand against his chest, breaking the kiss. "But I have one condition," I say.

Looking questioningly at me, he asks, "A condition?"

I nod. "We have to find a way to tell him. When the time is right, I want him to know about us. I don't want to be a secret forever, and I don't want him to find out the wrong way."

He searches my face for a moment before agreeing, and just knowing I have his support on my condition settles the nerves in my stomach.

CHAPTER 21
REID RATHE

"AREN'T you worried that Dustin will come visit Ivy or something?" Avery asks as we park my car at the diner.

The diner is busy tonight, which isn't surprising. It's not far from campus, and it's common for college kids to come after a long day of classes and studying. Dustin, Jacob, and I used to come here a lot when we were hungover and needed something greasy like burgers or bacon or bacon on burgers. We haven't been here for a while though. None of us gets so wasted that we have terrible hangovers anymore. None that requires grease, anyway.

"There's always that risk," I say with a laugh. She's so worried that she's biting on her nails while staring wide-eyed at the bright diner windows that splash light across the parking lot.

"Maybe we shouldn't tempt fate. We've only been dating for a week, and—"

I grab her hands and pull them from her mouth, kissing the back of her knuckles. "Our entire relationship is a risk."

"Yes! And we shouldn't chance it with a public date."

I twist my lips to the side, trying to think of how I can soothe her worries. "How about this: We go, we eat, we talk, and if Dustin shows up, we'll just tell him we're friends getting to know each other."

"And if he catches us kissing?"

Amusement crosses my face. "If it'll make you feel better, I won't even hold your hand."

She thinks about it for a moment before nodding. "Okay."

"Come on, let's get a booth." We get out of the car, and immediately I'm assaulted with the scent of bacon and syrup. The diner is famous for its pancakes, so I'm not surprised that it reaches all the way to the parking lot.

I place my hand at the small of her back and guide her into the diner. Once we're inside, we're immediately seated by a bored-looking hostess who probably wishes she was anywhere but at work. Sitting across from each other, we take the offered menus from the hostess, even though I'm pretty sure that neither one of us needs it.

She leaves, and I set my menu down. "Do you know what you're getting?"

She nods and slides her menu to the edge of the table. I set mine on top, and we place our elbows on the table and smile when Ivy slides up to us, a pad and pen in her hands.

A look of surprise crosses her face. "You're here? Both of you?"

I nod. "We wanted pancakes."

"Is this…" Ivy's gaze shoots back and forth between the two of us. "A date?"

Avery blushes but says, "It might be."

She glances around as if Dustin might pop out at any moment. "Isn't this kinda—I don't know—bold of you two?"

I raise my eyebrows at her. "Is Dustin coming tonight?" She shakes her head. "Then we're fine."

Blowing out a breath, she raises her pad of paper and poises her pen. "Your funeral. What are you two having?"

We order our pancakes, both with whipped cream topping, and two waters, and she shakes her head at us, mumbling to herself as she heads toward the kitchen.

I turn my attention back to Avery. The blush still sits on her cheeks, and I want more than anything to reach across the table and press my lips to the stained red of her skin. Instead, I start a conversation, hoping it takes her mind off of getting caught. The last thing I want is for her to feel uncomfortable with me. "Did your professors talk about a summer internship yet?"

"Yeah," she says, tucking a hair behind her ear. "I'm all nerves about it. I haven't worked since high school, and that was at a grocery store. I have no idea what I'll be like in a hospital setting, let alone where it might be. I can't afford to spend a summer in another city just for an internship."

"Maybe you'll get a paid internship."

"Yeah, maybe. Have you thought about where you're going to apply?"

I shrug a little. "I have a few places I wouldn't mind interning at. My mother certainly has her opinions on the matter."

At the mention of my mom, she leans a little into the table. Ivy sets our drinks in front of us, but that doesn't steer Avery from her question. "What do your parents do anyway?"

"They own a real estate company." Her eyebrows start to wiggle, and I try to hold in my laugh. "What are you doing?"

She frowns. "Trying to raise one eyebrow like Ivy. Did it work?"

I chuckle. "No. Not at all."

Waving a hand in front of her, she grumbles, "Whatever." She straightens her shoulders and sits up higher. "They must have a big company to afford everything they have."

I like that she didn't imply that it was my money too. It means I was right about her. She's not after what I'll inherit, and that warms a place in my chest. "Yeah, it's quite large. They were disappointed when I told them I was going to school for anesthesiology. They wanted me to learn the family business."

"Why didn't you want to?"

I pick up my drink and take a sip as I think of the answer. "I wasn't interested in what they do. And I wanted to make my own way in the world. I told them as much as well."

"And how'd that go?"

"Well, my mom wasn't happy, that's for sure."

She puckers her lips. "Your mom sounds controlling."

I nod slowly and set my drink back down. "She is, but she has her reasons. She only wants what's best for me, and after my last breakup, she's even more uptight about letting me do my own thing."

"Hmm," she hums before wetting her bottom lip. "What happened with your last girlfriend?"

My eyebrows rise. I never thought she'd ask about a past relationship. For a minute there, I watched her fight with herself over doing so. "It was a toxic relationship. She was pretty on the outside, but I quickly learned that looks weren't everything. She was ugly on the inside. She spent a lot of time getting close to my parents, but my mother saw right through her. She knew she was after their money, especially when she started talking about marriage."

"Oh," is her only answer. She glances down at her hands cupping her drink. And I don't know if it was perfect timing or bad timing because Ivy comes with our pancakes and sets them in front of us, along with a tiny pitcher of syrup.

"Need anything else, guys?" she asks, hands on her hips. We both shake our heads. "Well, enjoy."

She walks away without another word, and I watch her go, but when I look back at Avery, she's staring a little too hard.

"What?" I ask tentatively as I begin to dig into my food.

"You know I don't care about your family's money, right?"

I pause with the fork halfway to my mouth. "Of course I know that."

"Good," she says, breathing a sigh of relief.

"I know you're a genuine person. And I know that you don't really like that my family has a lot of money. You're good, baby girl."

At the nickname, she smiles a little and starts to cut up her pancakes. "Let's talk about something else."

And we do. We spend the next hour talking about random things from our childhoods, just getting to know one another on a deeper level. And when it's time to go home, I pay the check and kiss her at the apartment building's entrance before we part ways for the night.

CHAPTER 22
AVERY MOORE

"WHAT MOVIE ARE WE WATCHING ANYWAY?" I ask Ivy as I slip on a pair of my fuzzy socks. My toes are freezing, and the colder weather isn't helping. I mean, my toes are usually cold, but lately, as night falls, they turn into toesicles.

Reid and Dustin are coming over for a movie night. It was their idea since we all have class tomorrow. Ivy's already expressed her doubts about Reid and me being able to hide our dating status throughout an entire movie, but I want to see Reid, so I'm the one who agreed for both of us.

Reid and I have been dating for a full three weeks now, sneaking around and going on secret dates throughout the weeks. Dustin often asks where he's been but then shoos it off, thinking that he's got a girlfriend in the building. When he said that, I blanched, but Reid later told me that Dustin has thought that all along and had no idea that it was me.

I've never been in a relationship that's been so romantic before. I'm truly falling for this guy, and I can't stop it from happening. Not that I want to. What we're doing is the stuff of fairytales, and I almost—almost—forget that we're hiding the entire thing from Dustin the whole time. That's what Reid does. He makes me forget. He makes me feel like me, the truest me. And he worships me, both in bed and figuratively.

"Some horror movie of some kind," she grumps.

"Whose idea was that?" I squeak. I've never been a horror fan. They leave me unable to sleep for days afterward, thinking the shadows of my bedroom are hiding ghosts inside them.

"Theirs," she grumbles as she heads to the front door when knuckles rap against it.

I follow her out and laugh when the knocking becomes a tune. "We're coming!"

Ivy unlocks the door and swings it open, huffing as she does so. Reid and Dustin are wearing huge grins and come inside as if they own the place. Reid is carrying a couple of two-liter bottles of soda in his hands, and he passes them off to Ivy.

"Avery," Reid greets, his eyes sweeping my body, taking in my pajamas and ridiculous socks. When his gaze flicks back to mine, there's heat in them, and it makes me blush hardcore. "How are you?"

"Fine," I murmur, taking note of how Dustin is watching our exchange. "How about you?"

Dustin slaps Reid on the shoulder. "Dude bench pressed a new self-record today. You should have seen it. It was badass."

Reid wears a lazy grin at the praise. "Hard work pays off."

"That it does," Dustin says.

"Dustin, come help me pour the drinks!" Ivy calls from the kitchen. I hear the ice maker on the fridge whirring and knocking the ice around.

Dustin immediately takes off, and I turn to Reid. "You can't look at me like that tonight."

"Like what?"

I poke him in the chest and hiss. "Like you're stripping me naked with your eyes."

He wets his bottom lip. "If only that were possible."

The chuckle that rumbles out of his chest is sexy when I slap his arm playfully.

Dustin and Ivy return from the kitchen with our drinks in their hands. They pass Reid and me each one of our own, and then we head into the living room and find seats on the couches. They sit on one couch, and we sit on the other while we each set our drinks on the coffee table between them.

I try not to fidget with how close Reid is sitting, but I can feel his body warmth, and I want nothing more than to lean into it. The desire to cuddle is strong, but Dustin, even though he seems completely unaware, would definitely notice.

So instead, I snatch a blanket that's draped over the back of the couch and snap it over my body. I squeak when Reid captures a side of it and covers himself too. Realizing what he just did, we both glance at Dustin, but he's completely unaware, flicking through the apps on the TV. Ivy, on the other hand, witnessed the whole thing, and her eyes are narrowed as she mouths some sort of reprimand.

Huffing when she's finished, she asks the room, "Do we have to watch horror?"

She and Dustin bicker back and forth about it, but I don't pay attention to it because, under the blanket, Reid is reaching for me. His hand is sliding up my leg until it rests right next to my pussy and squeezes the skin there. Immediately, my body lights on fire. Still, Dustin seems unaware that I'm almost cuddling his best friend under the covers, and that best friend is laying on the moves.

He begins drawing small circles, inching closer to my pussy with each pass of his fingers. A small smirk settles on his face when I bite my bottom lip to hold in any sounds that I might involuntarily make.

Slowly, he turns his head to look at me fully. I can't help but return the stare, and we share that moment of silent communication, the one we always do where we don't need to actually say anything. I could look forever in his eyes. I could just get lost in them, and as the seconds tick by, I start to.

"Popcorn!" Ivy shouts, snapping our stare. Reid immediately lets go of my thigh as if we've been caught, and if the narrowed expression on Ivy's face is anything to go by, she did catch us.

"What?" Reid asks after a moment.

"We need popcorn." She turns to Dustin. "Do you have any?"

"Yeah," Dustin says, rubbing the back of his neck. "I think we have a bag of puffed popcorn."

"Good," she says, standing up and pulling him to his feet. "Come on, lover boy. Let's go get it."

Dustin frowns as she steers him from the apartment, and when he's out of earshot, she whips around with her finger jabbing in our direction. "You have a few seconds to get it out of your system, and when we come back, you're going to act normal. Got it?"

With that said, she leaves and shuts the door.

We're on each other immediately, lips clashing in a heated kiss. I gather myself on my knees and press my body into his. His hands roam my backside, and mine grip his shirt tightly in my fists. God, his hands feel like heaven. His touch turns me on and makes me feel safe at the same time.

Our tongues sweep over each other's, and we make little urgent sounds into our mouths. And when we hear Dustin's apartment door shut, we fly off of each other, quickly straightening our shirts and the blanket across our laps which had almost fallen to the floor.

My apartment door opens, and they both step through. A look of relief appears on Ivy's face, and she gives me a little nod, one that I return, letting her know that we'll behave for the rest of the night.

And we do. The only thing we do under the blanket is hold hands. I barely even notice the movie because I'm too busy relishing the fact that this man beside me is mine.

CHAPTER 23
REID RATHE

RAIN PELTS the windows as Jacob hops off the treadmill and joins me stretching on the mats. The gym is still pretty empty. Most students are still in class, but mine was canceled. Today is Jacob's short day, so it was a given to invite him to join me in an extra workout.

The smell of the gym and the sounds of the equipment being used soothes me. I'm a bundle of anxiety ever since Avery agreed to date me. I don't want to let her down. I don't want to give her a reason to end it because this girl is it for me. I know that with certainty. I fought for her, and now I have her, and I'm not going to let her go.

My phone goes off, and I grab it off the floor from beside me.

I grin at Avery's name and then open it up. As quickly as I open it, I just as quickly press the screen to my chest and peek at Jacob to see if he saw the screen. It was a picture of Avery naked in front of her mirror.

Seeing that he's engrossed in his leg stretches, I peel the phone away from my chest and get a second look. My cock stirs to life at the sight of her, and I have to start counting in my head so that it doesn't get full mast.

Me
That was…wow.

She sends a devil emoji.

Me
I'm definitely saving that to my phone.

Her
Or, you can just come over after class and see me naked for yourself.

I smirk.

Aren't you in class?

Her
Yes, and it's boring.

Me
When did you take the picture then?

Her
This morning. I debated all day about sending it.

Me
Well it made my day ten times better.

Her
Having a bad day?

Me
No, just a long one. I miss you.

Her
I miss you too.

"Who are you talking to?" Jacob asks, trying to peer over at my screen.

"I'll give you one guess," I say, setting my phone back down when she doesn't say anything else.

He shakes his head and stretches out his shoulders. "I don't even know why I ask."

I chuckle under my breath. "We're…uh…dating."

He stops stretching and whips his head to face me. "Dude."

"I know."

His fingers wiggle in my direction, tickling the air between us. "Avery and Reid. Together at last."

"You're an idiot," I say as I bat his hand away.

He laughs. "So what did Dustin say?"

I grimace and rub at the back of my neck. "Haven't told him."

For a minute, he just stares at me, a rare look of seriousness on his face. "He's going to freak out when he finds out."

"I know," I breathe.

"Just tell him before this gets messy and you drag all of us into it."

"I will," I say with more confidence than I feel. "When the time is right."

"Dude," he grumbles. "The time was right when you fucked her the first time because I'm going to assume there was a second time."

Guilt clings to the lining of my stomach. "We're in deep shit, aren't we?"

He nods. "Yes, and you're taking Ivy and me with you for knowing."

I sigh and crack my neck. "Just give me time to figure

out how to tell him. I will, I promise. We can't sneak around forever, nor do we want to remain a secret."

"Okay," he grumbles.

"Okay? That's it? Nothing snarky?"

"No snarky here today. I have my own issues."

I glance at him as I stand. He follows me to the weights. As I lay down on my bench press, he goes behind me to spot me. "Girl issues?"

His top lip curls. "Something like that."

"Is this that one girl?"

He nods. "She wants more."

"And what's wrong with that?"

"I've never had a relationship before," he admits. "I wouldn't even know where to begin with one."

"But you like her?"

He shrugs, but I can tell it's a bigger deal than what he's letting on. "Yeah, I suppose."

"Man, just do it. You like her; she likes you. Take the next step. Don't make this complicated like Avery and my relationship."

"What if it ends badly?" he asks after a moment.

"Aw," I coo. "Is Jacob worried about his heart?"

He rubs at his chest. "Yeah, I mean, I've never…this is new to me. I don't want any organs hurting."

I laugh and sit up. "Welcome to relationships. Shit hurts sometimes, but most of the time, it's the best thing that's ever happened to you."

"I'll take your word for it," he grumbles.

As I stand up, I glance at the time. Talking about relationships only makes me want to see her more, and if I hurry, I can get there on time.

I start to walk away. "Hey! Where are you going?" Jacob asks.

I turn and walk backward. "It's raining."

"Yeah, it has been for the last hour. What about it?"

Grinning at him, I say, "The best thing that's ever happened to me is about to get out of class and walk home in it."

Understanding crosses his face, and he rolls his eyes. "So you're going to pick her up instead?"

I dip my chin in confirmation and turn back around, giving him a small wave. As soon as I get to the locker rooms, I quickly shower, get dressed, and head out into the storm. Rain pelts my back as I race to my car.

It takes only minutes for me to get to her building, and I spot her right away, holding her backpack above her head to shield herself from the rain. I pull up to the side of the road and honk my horn.

She looks at me, and grateful reassurance overtakes her face as she makes a mad dash to the passenger side. Dropping her backpack at her feet, she quickly shuts the door and breathes a sigh of relief. "You didn't have to pick me up," she says, out of breath.

I pull away from the curb and turn on the heat when she starts to shiver. Despite her backpack, half of her is soaked. "I wasn't going to let you walk in this."

Goose bumps rise over her skin, and she crosses her arms over her chest for added warmth. "Don't you have a class?"

I shake my head. "The professor was sick today."

"Convenient," she murmurs.

Chuckling under my breath, I switch the topic. "Where are we headed?"

"My place."

I steer the car in that direction, and it takes less than a minute to pull into the parking lot. I park the car, and we both groan as the wind begins to pick up, pushing the rain nearly sideways. In a bout of shared bravery, we quickly pick up our bags, get out of the car, and race to the building's door. Once we're inside, we start to laugh, and I quickly steal a kiss from her wet lips.

Taking her hand, I drag her up the stairs. When we're at her door, I start to go inside her apartment, but she stops me with a tug of her hand in mine. "What are you doing?" she hisses, looking back at my apartment door.

"Coming with," I say with raised eyebrows, and then I wiggle them suggestively. "You promised I'd get to see you naked."

She looks around nervously, and I relax a little as I add, "He's still in class."

She bites her bottom lip. "Are you sure?"

I nod, push the door open, and close it behind us. Water droplets fall everywhere when I shake my wet hair. Glancing around, I ask, "Ivy?"

"Still in class too."

"Good." I take her to the bathroom, and when we're inside, we drop our bags near the vanity and kick off our shoes. Quietly, I shut the door and turn on the shower.

I start to strip out of my clothes but pause when she asks, "What are you doing?"

"*We* are going to shower. You're freezing." I take off my jeans and underwear and then go to her. She's nervously pulling at her fingers, and I seize them, plant a kiss on her knuckles, and then lift her soaked shirt over her head.

Steam starts to billow out over the curtain as I grab my phone from my bag and start the playlist I listen to when I do homework. I set it on the counter, and when I turn around, she's stepping into the shower. I hear her soft moan as the water hits her cold skin. Smiling, I follow her in and circle my arms around her middle, sharing the spray.

She rests the back of her head against my chest and asks, "Where do you see yourself in five years?"

I chuckle under my breath, surprised by the random question. "I don't know. With my degree and a good job, I guess married. Maybe a kid on the way."

Drawing small circles on my hand, she says, "Married to someone famous."

"Definitely," I joke before kissing the top of her head. "In all seriousness, I see you wearing my ring."

She hums in agreement. "So I fit into your future?"

I frown. "Of course you do. Avery. I wouldn't have been chasing you if I didn't see a future in us. Okay?" She nods against me. "Where's this coming from?"

She shrugs a little. "I just wanted to make sure this wasn't, like…a fling or something. I wanted to see if you were as serious about us."

I squeeze her a little. "Dead serious. Are you?"

Her wet hair sticks to my chest as she nods against me again. She circles in my arms and wraps her own around my neck. "I am."

Grinning mischievously down at her, I ask, "Should I get down on one knee now?"

She slaps my chest playfully. She opens her mouth to say something, but a knock sounds at the door. "Avery?" Dustin's voice calls through.

We both freeze.

"I thought he was in class, I swear," I murmur to her.

For a moment, we say and do nothing but hold our breath. The knock sounds again. "Avery, are you in there?"

She clears her throat. "I'm showering!"

"Obviously," we hear him grumble. "Have you seen Reid?"

She looks up at me, her eyes wide with fear. I give her an encouraging squeeze. "No," she lies. "Why?"

"His car is parked outside, but he's not at the apartment."

"The gym," I whisper to her.

"Maybe he's at the gym," she shouts.

"Yeah, maybe," he murmurs. "Okay, I'll talk to you later."

"Okay," Avery squeaks.

We listen to his footfalls fade down the hall until the apartment door shuts, and we both release the pent-up breath and sag into each other's arms. "That was close," I murmur.

She nods. "Should I have not lied?"

I kiss her, a soft and small slide of my lips over hers. "I would have backed you up with whatever you said."

As she nibbles on her bottom lip, I watch her mind work, watch as the guilt slithers over her features. "I should have told him."

I shake my head. "Him finding out about us while we're literally in the shower, naked, together isn't the way he should find out. He deserves more than that. You did the right thing." I grab the shampoo, squeeze some into my hand, and start massaging it into her hair. Her eyes close in bliss as I say, "We'll find a way to tell him."

"Okay," she murmurs as I tip her head into the shower's spray and rinse the suds out, and it's then I realize that she trusts me to make this okay. It's a lot to live up to, but we will figure this out. I'll do anything for this girl. I'll overturn the world for her, and if that means that I have to tell her brother alone so the wrath isn't put on her, I will.

CHAPTER 24
REID RATHE

MY CAR ROARS as I pull up to my parents' estate's circular driveway, the sound bouncing off the house's brick walls. Dustin likes to call my family's home a mansion. As I park the car and stare up at it, I suppose that it is. There are eleven bedrooms and thirteen bathrooms, way more room than what's needed for a family of three, but my parents like to live extravagantly. Always have and always will.

Hell, my mother has joked many times about being buried with her jewelry, but I secretly think she's being one-hundred percent serious.

My mother called me here for lunch, and since it's Saturday and there are no classes on the weekend, I had no excuse to get out of it. I know what she wants. She thinks that I've had time to think over everything I said to her last time. That I've had a moment to reconsider my arranged marriage with Dorothy.

I honestly thought I put an end to this. I was so sure that the subject would be dropped, but I should have never guessed that my mother would let that slide. This marriage means too much to her.

The sun shines brightly in my car, and the autumn leaves swirl around the gardener, who is trying to rake them up on the east side of the house. Ever since the rainstorm, the temperature has plummeted, bringing a chill to the atmosphere. Autumn will forever remind me of Avery because, just last night, I snuck her out and took her for an evening picnic, laid her in the leaves, and kissed her under the sunset. The way her scent complemented the smell of autumn will forever be etched into my mind.

I sigh and look back at the house, at the towering three stories. Pulling on my college sweater, I step out of my car and make my way up the steps. I almost knock on the door because this house represents a home that is no longer *my* home. I am not the same person I was when I left for college two years ago, and I'm certainly not the son they thought they raised.

Heading inside, I call out my mom's name and shut the door, listening for her response.

The house cleaner pops her head out of the office with a duster in her hand and greets me with a warm smile. She's been with our family since I was a young child, except, when I was younger, I don't remember all the gray hair. She's always had it tied in a tight bun, though. She's wearing simple jeans and a plain T-shirt, and the skin around her eyes wrinkles with her grin.

"Reid," she greets. "Welcome home."

I clear my throat a little, not bothering to correct her. "Hi, Sarah. Are my parents home?"

She nods and points her duster down the hallway that leads to the kitchen. "Just follow your nose. I baked some cookies for you, and they're waiting on the counter."

"Macadamia nut?" I ask, feeling slightly better about having my favorite treat on hand for whatever my mother wants.

Her smile grows, and she taps her temple. "I'll never forget it."

I touch her shoulder as I pass her. "Thanks."

"Any time, dear. Say goodbye to me before you leave."

"I will," I agree, already halfway down the hall.

She was right. I can smell the cookies from here and follow the trail of them. Once I enter the grand kitchen, I nod to my father, who is reading the newspaper at the white marble island. I head around it and straight to my mother who is sorting the takeout boxes. I press a kiss to my mother's cheek, and she leans into it, patting my shoulder in thanks.

"How was the drive?" she asks as I snatch a cookie from the plate settled on her right. My parents' estate is a thirty-minute drive from campus.

"Windy," I answer honestly around a mouthful. Cookie crumbles fall to my sweater, and I brush them off as I stuff the rest of it into my mouth.

She takes the takeout boxes to the large dining hall and sets each of our meals down on the massive table. My father follows me, and the chair legs scrape against the wood floor as we pull them out and take a seat. Grabbing a fork, she asks, "And school?"

Opening my box and picking up my own fork, I say, "Harder than last year. How's work?"

My parents own several grand apartment and condo buildings, all acquired because they own the largest real estate company this side of the country. They built it from the ground up. Nothing was inherited, and I always admired them for it. What I don't admire now is how they flaunt their money. Hell, my fork is gold. I grimace about it as I take a bite of my sweet and sour chicken.

My mother's eyes light up. "We just bought out Echo Realty, actually."

I raise my eyebrows. "That's what, the third real estate company you've taken over?"

She waves a hand in the air. "I don't keep track, dear. Accomplishments are accomplishments, and goals are goals." Under her breath, she adds, "You'd know if you had any."

My father grumbles a warning, saying her name.

"It's fine, Dad."

Her head whips to me, and she narrows her eyes, and I know the real reason for me being here is about to begin. "It's not fine. You could have chosen any college you wanted to, but you chose Smithson University. You could have gone to Harvard. You had the acceptance letter in your hand, and you just threw it away."

I shrug and lean back in my seat, my food looking unappetizing now. "It didn't feel right."

And honestly, if asked if I'd ever change my mind, I wouldn't in a heartbeat. I made the right call. That school wasn't for me, and I knew it even then, an eager high school graduate.

"Well, we can't all go on our gut feelings. Look how that turned out with your last girlfriend."

I sigh and pinch the bridge of my nose. "When are you going to let that go?"

She points at me. "You let her destroy you, and she almost destroyed this family. Think what would have happened if you'd have married her."

Flicking my gaze back to hers, I pin her with a stare. "But I didn't, so the point of this conversation is …?"

"We didn't call you here to fight," my father interjects.

"Then what did you call me here for?"

After a moment, my mother takes a deep breath and releases it with a smile. She settles her posture and says, "Dorothy's parents would like to move the wedding up to next summer. Oh, and they found the perfect venue. You should see the view and the -"

I slam my hand on the counter. "I am *not* marrying her."

My mother startles and has the audacity to look at me with a shocked expression. Once the shock clears from my outburst, she whispers fervently, "It's been arranged."

"Then unarrange it because I will *not* be waiting at the altar for her."

"Reid," she presses.

I shake my head. "I don't love her, Mom. She's not the one I love. I won't marry someone I don't love."

My parents are silent for a moment until my dad breaks it. "But you do love someone?"

It's a no-brainer for me, and I immediately nod. "She's great. You'd like her."

"What's her name?" he asks.

"Avery Moore."

My mom gasps and places her hand over her heart. "Dustin's sister? Reid, now, see reason. They come from a poor family. This will end exactly like your last fling, and it won't be pretty."

I shake my head. "She's not after the family money, Mom."

"You can't know that for certain."

"I do, actually. She's not like that."

"Reid—" my mother begins, setting her fork down to give me a lecture.

I beat her to it, standing up from the table and preparing myself to leave. This isn't worth it. "I know the family, Mom. They're not like that, and neither is she. They couldn't care less about money and inheritances. All they want is what's best for each other."

"Don't leave, son," my father asks of me.

"I'm not going to sit here and listen to this." I look directly at my mother. "I won't marry Dorothy. I don't give you permission to rule my life anymore. I'm a grown man, and I get to decide what I do with my life, and if that means marrying someone with less money and making your image look bad, then so be it."

I turn and walk away, but the smallness of my mother's voice has me pausing. "Do we at least get to meet her?"

Looking over my shoulder, I see the plea in my mother's eyes. My heart softens a little bit. "When the time is right, I'll bring her over."

And then I leave, stomach still empty and my mood soured. I wave goodbye to Sarah and thank her again for the cookies, and then I head back to campus to be with the one and only person I want to see right now: my girl.

CHAPTER 25
AVERY MOORE

"THIS PUNCH IS SPIKED, isn't it..." I ask Ivy as she dips the ladle into the bowl of red liquid and scoops a generous amount into our cups.

"Yes." She glances up at me with a grin so wide I almost consider taking her drink. She's had double the amount that I've had, and she's definitely feeling it. "You're going to drink it, and you're going to *like it.*"

I chuckle as she eagerly passes me the drink, and I take a sip. It really is too delicious to even be legal at this point. I can't even taste the alcohol, though I'm sure there's a generous amount in it.

There are a few people behind us waiting for the punch bowl so we step aside, leave the kitchen, and head into Jacob's living room. Jacob lives in an apartment complex on the other side of campus. We had to drive here, but thankfully, Reid said he wouldn't be drinking tonight so he can drive us home.

His place is the typical bachelor pad - leather couches, dark colors - and he's lucky enough to have a roommate that parties as well. His roommate is on the football team, and they're celebrating a win. I don't watch football, but

I'm happy our school is good at sports. However, that means this place is packed, and squeezing between the people without spilling my drink is proving difficult.

Ivy steers us to Dustin and Jacob, who hover by the stereo. I frown. When we left them to refill our drinks, Reid was with them. It's just the two of them now, and I scan the crowd for him, but with so many heads and a little alcohol in my system, I don't spot him right away.

"Where's Reid?" I whisper-yell in Ivy's ear.

She glances around, and when she doesn't spot him, she shrugs. "Want me to ask?"

I shake my head. That would seem desperate, and though we had a close call at getting caught the other day, I don't want another close call.

The two boys laugh at something they shared and turn to us as we crowd closer. Jacob smiles at me, takes in my dress, and whistles. "You look hot tonight, Avery."

Dustin slaps him in the stomach, and he bends over, clutching his abdomen. "No hitting on my sister."

A blush creeps up my neck anyway, and I take a drink to hide that fact.

"Don't you have a girl or something now anyway?" Ivy points out.

Jacob rights himself and gives Dustin an accusatory look. "You told her?"

Ivy waves a hand around. "We tell each other everything."

Not everything, I correct in my head. But with any luck, Dustin will never know the secret she's kept.

"So where is she?" Ivy asks, getting up on her tiptoes and looking around.

Sheepishly, Jacob glances down at his feet, tucking his lips between his teeth.

"She's not here," Dustin says for him. "I already asked."

"Where the hell is she?" Ivy presses with a deep frown.

Dustin slaps Jacob on the shoulder. "My man is afraid of commitment."

"I didn't invite her because I didn't want to give her the wrong impression."

Ivy's eyes narrow. "And just think of the impression you're giving her by not inviting her at all."

Jacob cringes. "Why is this so complicated?"

"You're making it complicated," I answer, realizing how hypocritical I sound.

He gives me a look for a split second, one that tells me he is, in fact, thinking I'm being hypocritical.

I shrug, and he sighs. "How do I make it less complicated?"

"Do you like the girl?" Ivy asks.

He reluctantly nods as though he can't believe he's admitting it himself.

"Then start taking her places. Dates. Football games. Walk her to class. It's not that hard, Jacob."

Dustin rubs the back of his neck. "Sometimes you guys make it hard. Sometimes we don't know what the hell you want."

Ivy leans into the circle we've created and winks at them. "Sometimes we don't know what we want, either."

I laugh as they start to bicker back and forth and look around to see if I know any other faces. I see a couple of girls from my classes, but we aren't on friendship terms, so I don't bother going over and saying hello. There's a couple making out by the speaker on the other side of the room and beer pong going on in the dining room.

My perusal stops when I spot Reid, and I smile. He's leaning against the wall and…I scowl. He's talking to a girl. I don't recognize her at all, and since Reid, Dustin, Ivy, Jacob, and I run in the same circles, it'd be likely that

I'd know who he'd be having such an intense conversation with.

She laughs at something he says and touches his chest, and jealousy curls in my gut.

It's nothing. It's just a touch.

His hand comes up over hers, and he leans down and says something into her ear.

Okay, so maybe it's more than friends.

My face flushes, and tears spring to my eyes. I thought I could trust him, I thought I was the only girl he wanted to flirt with, but clearly, I was wrong. He lied to me, just like Neil. And to do it at the same party I'm at? It's the ultimate betrayal.

My heart cracks and the tears begin to spill. I have to get out of here, and before I know it, I'm passing Ivy my drink and pushing through the crowd. Unfortunately, Reid and the girl are by the door, and I try not to look at them as I pass them.

Reid's attention catches on me as I rush by, and he calls out my name. I ignore it and quickly exit the apartment. Jacob lives on the third floor, so I make quick work of getting down the first flight of steps before I hear Reid call my name again as he tries to keep up with me.

"No!" I say when he asks me to wait.

I make it to the first floor and rush toward the door. Cold air greets me and licks at the fresh tears on my cheeks. I begin to power walk on the sidewalk, which is difficult in heels, but no matter how fast I go, Reid's strides are longer.

He snags me by the elbow and spins me to face him. "What is wrong?" he asks, taking in my tears with concern.

I look away from him and yank my arm out of his grasp.

"Avery?" he presses, stepping closer to me. "Why are you crying? Why are you running from me?"

Whipping my gaze back to his, I pin him with a murderous stare. "You know, I thought you were different, Reid. But you're just like every other guy."

He frowns. "What are you talking about?"

I throw my hands in the air. "I saw you flirting with that girl."

His eyes go wide, and for a second, he says nothing. "Are you talking about Dorothy?"

"Oh, is that her name?" I ask sarcastically.

"She's just a friend, Avery," he whispers in shock.

"It looked more than friendly to me," I grumble, losing my fight because it's happening all over again.

He reaches for my face and cups both of my cheeks so that my attention is solely on his eyes. "I've known Dorothy since we were kids. It's a long story, and I'm not going to lie to you, but my parents wanted us to get married."

Fresh tears fall as I whisper, "So you're engaged?"

He shakes his head. "I told my parents that I refuse to marry her, that I had someone else that I loved. I was telling Dorothy that tonight, and we agreed to remain friends and only friends."

I freeze in his arms. "Love?"

A smile spreads across his face, and he rubs his thumbs over my wet cheeks. "You caught that, did you?"

"You love me?" I ask, the anger slowly fading as shock takes over.

He nods and waits patiently for me to come to terms with the fact that he said the 'L' word first. "I've wanted to tell you for a while now, but I wasn't sure if you felt the same, all things considered. I wanted to give you time before I bombarded you with that declaration. But it slipped out, and I can't take it back and -"

"You love me," I repeat more for myself than for him.

"You're panicking, aren't you." He lets go of my cheeks and rubs at his jaw.

I shake my head and wipe away my tears. "I love you too, Reid."

His gaze flicks back to mine, and he searches my face for the lie. When he finds none, he wraps an arm around my middle and tugs me to him. "You do?" he asks, his forehead on mine.

I nod, new tears for a completely different reason gathering in my eyes.

He takes my mouth, kissing me deeply, and I melt into him.

This is a big step for me, admitting I found love in another man. A man who is honorable. Trustworthy. A man I second-guessed because I saw something I thought meant one thing but was another.

I never said I wasn't an idiot sometimes.

We kiss under the autumn moon and the stars that twinkle around it, the breeze rustling the leaves our only song. I love him. I do. And I pour it into my kiss.

He tugs me closer, and his erection hits my belly button. His hands roam my back, and I wrap my arms around his neck, pulling on the hair at the nape.

Out of breath, he breaks the kiss, grabs my hand, and takes me into the parking lot. "Where are we going?" I ask.

He doesn't answer me. Instead, he heads to his car, opens it, and pushes the passenger seat back. The gears in the seat whir until it comes to a complete stop. He takes a seat, unbuttons his pants, and pushes them down. My eyes go wide when he pulls me onto his lap, my dress riding up my thighs and bunching at my waist.

Gathering up on my knees, I shut the door, slide my thong aside, and don't waste any time sinking down onto him. We groan and I start riding him immediately. Desperate. Needy. A final union for our declaration. I can't get close enough to him, but I try when our lips find each other's once more.

His hands fall to my hips, guiding me, and mine find his chest, steadying myself as I rise and fall on him. We moan into each other's mouths, our breaths fanning against each other's cheeks. It doesn't take long for my abdomen to coil tight.

"I'm never letting you go," he whispers against my mouth.

"I know," I whisper back, and then I fall apart, my pussy clamping down and squeezing him tight. It's the strongest one I've ever had, and I break the kiss in ecstasy. His mouth works across my jaw and down my neck, and he moans deeply as he clamps his teeth on my shoulder and cums inside me.

When we're both spent, we rest our sweaty foreheads against each other. We chuckle under our breath, and I open my mouth to tell him something, but a knock on the window startles us both.

We look over and find Dustin standing there, a look of rage on his face.

"Shit," Reid whispers.

Dustin snarls at him, turns on his heel, and walks away. That's when I see Ivy standing a few feet away with a pained expression on her face.

CHAPTER 26
REID RATHE

"DUSTIN, WAIT!" I shout as he heads into the building. He says nothing, and I rip the closing door open and stomp after him. "Dustin!"

He whips around to face me. Face contorted in rage, he advances and punches me in the jaw so quickly that I didn't see it coming. "I said to leave her alone. I told you! And you didn't listen!"

I put up my hands, my jaw aching. "We were going to tell you—"

"When?" he shouts, his fists clenched at his sides. "Because I know my sister. She doesn't sleep around, Reid. This has been going on for a while, hasn't it?"

I look down at my feet and cross my arms over my chest. "Yes."

"That's what I thought," he growls. "Fuck you."

My gaze lifts to his with a frown. "Why is it so bad that I'm dating your sister?"

"Because!" He throws up his hands. "When—not if—you break up, I'll be forced to be in the middle. I'll have to choose: my best friend or my sister."

"We aren't going to break up."

He laughs without humor. "That's what everyone thinks."

"We love each other, man."

I was hoping that that statement would calm him, get him to see reason, but it just fuels his anger. His cheeks stain red. "I can't believe you. I thought we were friends, Reid. I thought I could trust you. And then you go behind my back."

He turns and starts to head up the stairs. "Dustin," I call after him.

He waves me off. "Leave, Reid. Fuck off."

And then he disappears up the next flight of steps, leaving me there reeling. What the fuck just happened? Did I lose my best friend?

I tug my hair, curse loudly, and kick the bottom step. My foot throbs as I turn around and leave the building, finding Avery and Ivy outside. How the hell did this go from the best night of my life to one of the shittiest?

Ivy has Avery in her arms as Avery sobs on her shoulder. I head toward them, fuming and feeling defeated at the same time.

Glancing up at me, Ivy asks, "How bad is it?"

"Bad," I say, looking straight at Avery. She lifts her head to return the gaze.

"Crap," Ivy breathes, letting go of Avery.

"What do we do?" Avery asks.

I shake my head and pull at the back of my neck. "I don't know."

Sighing, Ivy points to my car. "Take her home, Reid. I'll see if I can talk some sense into Dustin."

I nod, wish her luck, and take Avery to the car. We say nothing on the entire ride across the campus. Her sniffles nearly kill me, but I give her the silence she needs to process what just happened. Hell, I'm still processing it.

When we pull up to our apartment building, I help

her out of the car and guide her inside. We take the stairs slowly and reach the hallway that separates my apartment from hers. "Avery," I say, pulling her in close and tipping her chin so her eyes meet mine.

"I haven't seen him that mad since...oh god, he's going to hate me forever."

"You don't know that," I whisper.

"I do." The vulnerable look in her eyes is nearly my undoing. "I just lost my brother."

"Hey-hey-hey," I coo. "He'll come around."

She shakes her head and I drop my hand to her waist. "You may be his best friend, but you don't know him like I do. He doesn't change his mind often, especially when it's something he's passionate about."

"We'll figure this out," I try to console.

She shakes her head again and steps out of my arms. "We can't do this."

I frown at her. "Do what?"

Waving a hand between us, she says, *"This."*

"As in *us*?"

Sobbing once, she nods. "I can't lose my brother, and you can't lose your best friend. We have to end this."

My heart cracks in my chest. "Don't say that. Please, don't say that."

She bites her bottom lip and then angrily wipes at her tears. "It's our only option."

"But we love each other. You said so. You're just going to walk away from that?"

"I love my brother too! He's my brother, Reid. My brother!"

If someone cut me open and stole my heart, it would be less painful. I grip at my chest and squeeze, wanting to rip it out myself. "Please, don't, Avery. Don't say it."

She looks away from me, her jaw set. "I'm breaking up with you. This is where we end."

Tears prick my eyes, and I swear to God, my life just ended. The chase, the moments we shared, flash before my eyes until it reaches this one moment where she's walking away from me. From us.

"That's it? We're just done, like that?" I snap my fingers in emphasis.

"Yes," she says, still not looking at me. Her voice is toneless like she's detached from her body. "I'm sorry."

A tear falls down my cheek, and I want more than anything to go to her and try to get her to change her mind, but I know I won't. Dustin is family, and their family is tight. They mean the world to each other. And me? I'm on the outside.

Finally, she looks back at me. "Goodbye, Reid."

She doesn't wait for me to say anything before she's turning around and entering her apartment, shutting the door on me and what we shared. And just like that, I lost my girl and might have lost my best friend, all in one night.

CHAPTER 27
AVERY MOORE

I STARE at the text thread Reid sent me over the course of the last couple of days, rereading over and over again.

> **Him**
> Please reconsider. I'm begging you.
>
> I can't breathe without you, baby girl.
>
> Let me have one last kiss, Avery. Please.
>
> God, I miss you.

Today is the first day since I broke up with him that I've left my room for more than just the bathroom. My heart is broken, and I've spent the days crying against my pillow. This feels worse than Neil. This is a hole in my chest. An ache in my heart. Raw cheeks from crying too much. Bags under my eyes from rarely sleeping for fear of dreaming of him.

I don't know where to turn. I don't know what I'm doing anymore other than simply existing. I don't know who I am or how I got here.

Scratch that. I do know how I got here. I partook in a

forbidden romance, and it came back to bite me in the ass.

I should have seen this coming.

I should have saved myself the heartache and walked away from Reid when he caught me.

Fresh tears fall. No. I had a great love. I had something special, and for a while, I got to enjoy it. I'll always carry those memories, always carry him in my heart, even if it nearly kills me to hold him there, remembering what we shared for the rest of my life.

The front door opens, and I look up from my phone in the spot on the couch where I'm curled up.

Ivy walks in with a box of takeout food with the diner's logo on it. "Oh honey," she says, coming to me and kneeling before me. "You're crying again."

I sob. "I can't help it."

She grabs my phone that's still lit up and reads the texts. When she's finished, she looks at me with sad eyes. "This will blow over."

"No, it won't."

She tucks her hair behind my ear. "You'll find someone else."

"I don't want anyone else. I'm done. I'm never dating again."

She shushes me, snags the box of tissues off the coffee table, and dabs my cheeks with a Kleenex. "Don't say that."

I sit up, and she comes to sit beside me. "All I want is him."

Her lips twist to the side. "Dustin's still pretty angry. I don't think it's a good idea to go back to Reid. He's barely talking to anyone right now."

"Is he still mad at you?"

She blows out a breath. "He lets me cuddle now, so it's not too bad."

When Ivy went back into the party to try to talk some sense into Dustin, she admitted to knowing. He was so angry with her that she was worried their relationship was ending. Thankfully, that didn't happen.

"Is he going to kick Reid out?" That's the last thing I want. I broke up with him so that all of our relationships, aside from mine and Reid's, don't come to an end.

She shakes her head. "He won't admit it, but the fact that you guys aren't seeing each other has eased his rage on the matter."

"That kind of makes him a prick."

Sighing, she runs her hand through her hair. "Yeah. He's just really mad, and mad people do irrational things. He feels like he was betrayed."

I sniffle and look at my hands in my lap. "I'm glad he didn't end things with you."

She grabs my hand and folds her fingers through mine. "Me too. I was really worried there for a minute."

"You know I'm grateful that you kept our secret, right?"

She straightens her shoulders and declares, "Hos before bros, girlie. I got your back." Leaning, she pushes the takeout box closer to me. "Now, eat something."

"I can't."

"Girl, you're losing weight. This can't go on forever. It's unhealthy. You need to fuel yourself."

I stare at the box, knowing she's right. I'm not meaning to starve myself. I'm just not hungry, but I can't keep denying my body what it needs. "Is it pancakes?"

She smiles a little at me. "I told you, I got your back."

"I know you do," I say as I pluck up the box and bring it to my lap. I open it up and smile a little. There's whipped cream on top. "Are you trying to make me feel better?"

"Clearly it's working. You're at least smiling."

I grip the plastic fork, cut off a piece, and stuff it into my mouth. It tastes like ash, but I won't tell her that. She was thoughtful enough to bring it to me and take care of me when I need it most.

"Are you caught up on homework?" she asks, eyeing my backpack by the table.

I shake my head. "I've been a little preoccupied."

"What about your internship applications for the summer? Did you start those?"

"No," I admit.

She slaps my knee, stands up, and goes to get my backpack. "Then that's what we're doing tonight. We're not going to wallow. We're going to hold our heads up high. Okay?"

Swallowing, I nod. "I can try."

"Good." She sets my backpack in front of me.

CHAPTER 28
REID RATHE

I RUB at my eyes and slap my cheeks, trying to get myself to wake up. Tomorrow will be a full week that Avery and I haven't been together. The days bleed into the night, and I no longer know what day it is. If it wasn't for Jacob, I wouldn't be sitting here in Spanish class. He's really stepped up these last few days, coming over often to be the buffer between me and Dustin.

Dustin's slowly starting to talk to me again. More like, "Do you have grocery money?" or "Can you pass me the remote?" Little things, but it's progress, and knowing I didn't lose him forever at least gives me room to breathe.

I haven't told my parents about Avery, and I don't plan to. Ever. I won't give them the satisfaction of knowing that I'm going through another terrible heartbreak. I'll never hear the end of it, and then my mother will try to continue with the wedding. Just because Avery and I are no longer together, doesn't mean I want to marry Dorothy. Hell, at Jacob's party, she admitted to not wanting to marry me also.

So, to keep that part of my life behind me, I've

decided to never tell my parents. I gave Avery all of me, and in the end, it wasn't enough.

Jacob and I are sitting in our usual spot in Spanish, and I tap my pen as I watch the door for Avery to come in. I just want a glimpse. I just need to see her. It'll be enough to tide me over until next week. It has to be. And when the class ends indefinitely at the end of the semester? I can't even think about that. She was it for me. I'll always want her.

The lecture hall doors open at the same time the professor stands at the podium and begins the class. But I can't pay attention to that because Ivy and Avery sneak into the class and take seats in the back row.

I crane my neck to look at her. Her hair is in a messy bun, her sweatshirt is stained, and she looks like she hasn't slept in days. She's also lost weight, and that kills me, knowing she's suffering as much as me. I don't know what I expected when I saw her again, but I don't wish her to suffer. I want her to be happy even if it's not with me.

The professor continues to rattle on, but I keep sneaking glances behind me. Not once does she look in my direction. Not once does she acknowledge that I'm sitting here. I get it. It probably hurts too much. Hell, I can feel the pain wash through my own body.

After a while, I notice that her laptop hasn't been opened. She's just staring straight again, rigid.

I grab my phone from my backpack, open it up, and send her a text.

> Baby girl, you're not taking care of yourself.

I can hear her phone vibrate from down here. She picks it up and glances at the screen before setting it back down. I'm used to the unanswered texts. I can deal with them. What I can't deal with is the lack of expression, the lack of emotion. She's blocking them off, closing herself off to numb the pain.

Nibbling on my lip, I turn back to the professor. Minutes tick by, and I hear the lecture hall door shut. I turn back around and find the seat next to Ivy vacant. Ivy catches my eye, and her lips turn down in a sympathetic expression.

Every part of me wants to chase after her. Wants to hold her. Wants to tell her that we'll get through this, but instead, I stay seated. It would just make things harder, and I don't want this to be any harder than it already is.

ONE MONTH LATER...

Me
I'm thinking about you today. I think about you every day.

Sitting on the couch in my apartment, homework in my lap, I stare at the screen, at the text I sent an hour ago that's still gone unresponded to. I know she reads them, but she never responds.

Aside from Spanish, I haven't seen her for a month. Not even in the hallway. She goes to class and stays home. I've talked to Ivy about it, making sure she's eating and getting fresh air, and she always assures me that she's taking care of her and that she'll be like this for a little while.

Dustin comes out of his room, rubbing at his eyes. He stops in the hallway, and I look up at him. He just woke up from a nap, and his hair is in disarray. "You look like shit, dude," he says as he takes me in.

Every day that passes, he says more and more to me. He's even starting to go to the gym with me and Jacob again, a fact I'm grateful for. I still have my best friend even if it came at a great cost. We aren't the same, but at least we're headed in the right direction.

"Yeah," I say, scrubbing at the stubble that I barely bother to shave these days. I saw myself in the mirror this morning after I showered. I have dark circles under my eyes and have contemplated finding a remedy for that, aside from sleep, just so I don't look like such a mess.

He steps farther into the room, a look of guilt on his face, and I almost think he's going to say something heartfelt, but instead, he points at the TV. "Want to watch some football?"

I watch him and wonder at the guilt before I shake it off and move my textbooks aside for him to sit. "Sure," I answer. He takes a seat next to me and crosses an ankle over a knee. "You okay?"

He nods. "Yeah. You?"

No, I want to answer. But instead, I grab the remote and say, "Yeah."

CHAPTER 29
AVERY MOORE

FOUR MONTHS LATER

Him
Happy Birthday, baby girl.

I STARE at the screen while waiting in a stingy hospital office waiting room, sitting in the most uncomfortable chairs on the planet.

It's been a few weeks since Reid messaged me, and for a while there, I was healing. I didn't spend my nights crying. I wasn't rereading his texts. But now the message is there, waiting. Begging for me to reply just this once. It's my birthday, right? I can gift myself this.

Looking around the office, I scan the receptionist's desk full of files and little bobbles as I work to not shed a tear. He remembered, and that means so much to me. Do I say something back? Should I?

I clutch my phone a little tighter. No, I shouldn't. It would give him hope. Hell, it'd give *me* hope.

My brother has finally started laughing and joking with me again. It's not the same, but we're healing. I still have him, and I can't have those things if I give Reid and me hope. If I start something where I shouldn't.

Shutting off my phone, I slide it back into my purse and straighten my navy-blue pencil skirt. I need to stay focused. I have this interview and a few others over the course of the next few days for an internship for this summer. For the first two interviews I had, I didn't have any luck snagging the internship. Ivy says the sadness in my eyes is something I can't hide and that they pick up on it right away. No one wants a sad intern. The dark circles certainly don't help either. I probably look like I'm not capable of enduring the long and stressful days of an internship in a hospital setting.

I square my shoulders. But this interview will be different. I'll put on a smile even if it's forced. I will show them that I'd be a good fit. I have to. I have to carry on with my life. I have to try.

The office door opens, and a middle-aged man with black hair graying at the temples steps out with a smile on his face. "Ms. Moore?"

Breathing a sigh of relief for not sitting here and dwelling on my thoughts any longer, I stand and hold out my hand. He takes it in his warm and soft palm, the handshake firm, just like my father taught me. "I'd introduce myself properly, but my last name is hard to pronounce, so why don't you just call me George."

I curtly nod, let go of his hand, and shoulder my purse. "It's so nice to meet you, George. Thank you for seeing me."

"Of course." He gestures into his office, stepping aside so that I can enter. I take a look around, glancing at the books squatting on two bookcases, the standard hospital desk dividing the room, and the pictures that line the wall behind his desk.

"Please, take a seat," he says, gesturing for the orange

chairs in front of his desk while he strides across the room and settles in his office chair.

Adjusting the back of my skirt, I sit and set my purse at my feet. I fold my hands across my lap and nod to the pictures on the wall. "Is that your family?"

He shifts to look at the pictures then returns his attention to me. "It is. My wife and two daughters."

"You have a beautiful family," I compliment. "How old are your girls?"

"Olivia is five and Ariel is seven."

"Sounds like a fun age."

He nods. "At times. They're my pride and joy though. Both of them want to become doctors."

I smile at him though it doesn't reach its full potential. "Just like their dad, I bet."

He chuckles and beams with pride. "You bet ya." He then grabs a file on the left side of his desk and opens it up. I read my name on the tab and start to fidget. "I've read through your file and noticed you haven't worked since high school. Any reason?"

I clasp my hands tighter in my lap. The other two interviewers asked the same question, so I came prepared with the best answer I could possibly give. "Yes. I've been focused on my studies. They're my number one priority."

Smiling a little, he looks back at the file, shuffling papers around. "That's good. Studies are important. I—" His phone rings, and he holds up a finger while picking up the phone with his other hand. "Hello?" A brief pause and a long sigh. "Olivia, remember what Daddy said about calling while I'm at work if there isn't an emergency? Mommy can handle this problem. No, no, you tell Ariel that she needs to share. Okay, baby girl, Daddy will see you after work."

Baby girl. My throat clogs at the familiar sentimental word, and in my head, I hear it in Reid's voice, in that loving way that pulled at my heart. Two simple words that meant more to me when I needed to hear them most.

I swallow, trying to get the lump out of my throat, but it just won't budge, and before I know it, tears are clouding my vision.

He hangs up the phone and starts to say something, but when he glances at me, he frowns. "Are you okay, Ms. Moore?"

I lift my hand to my mouth, and a sob escapes into my palm. Waving him off with my other hand, I choke out, "I'm fine."

"You don't look fine. Is it something I did?"

I wave him off again. "No, no."

I sob again. Jesus, why can't I get it together?

Baby girl. I really can't function without him. When will this get easier? When will I be able to move on? It's been four months!

He leans forward and rests his elbows on his desk. "Ms. Moore…" He clears his throat. "I'm going to be real honest with you. You seem like a nice woman, but I get the feeling you're…"

"A mess?" I laugh without humor and wipe away tears.

"Well…yes. I'd love to have you as an intern, but I just don't think you're ready."

I drop my hands back to my lap and stare at my fingers. "But I need this internship."

He's quiet for so long that I steal a glance at him. His expression is one of sorrow. "I understand that," he says softly, passing me a few tissues. "But I know your head isn't in it. I don't think you'd be a good fit at this time."

Dabbing my eyes, I nod a little. "I understand," I say meekly.

He stands up from his desk, travels around it, and offers me a hand. I take it, and he helps me stand. "I don't know what's going on with you, but I'd advise you to sort it out before your next interview. Okay?"

I nod again, shoulder my purse with as much dignity as I can, and turn to him in the doorway. "Thank you for giving me a chance. I appreciate it."

His smile is sad as he ushers me out. "It was my pleasure. You take care of yourself."

As I walk through the halls of the hospital, I dig my phone back out of my purse and power it back on, anything to distract me from the hot mess that I've quickly become.

An incoming text comes immediately.

Him
Good luck today.

Fresh tears fall, and I rush out of the hospital as fast as I can, the scabs on my heart exposed and raw. It's then I know that I'll never be able to get over him. I just have to learn to live without him. Somehow.

CHAPTER 30
REID RATHE

FIVE MONTHS LATER

I WALK OUT OF MY PARENTS' house and pull my coat tighter around me as I head to my car. The spring's cold wind just won't relent today, but at least my visit with my parents went well. They congratulated me on my achieved internship at Joseph Children's Hospital. I don't necessarily want to work with just children, but their program is the best on this side of the country. It's a big achievement, getting accepted, and I walk with my head held up higher than I have in months.

My phone rings, and I dig it out of my back pocket, answering it without even looking at the screen. "Hello?"

"Hey, man," Dustin says. In the background, I can hear people talking, but it's muted as though he's in another room.

"Hey, what's up?"

Dustin's been at his parents' for a few days now, helping them remodel the kitchen, so it's just been me at the apartment. It's been lonely, but I've found things to do. I've taken up knitting. I'm terrible at it, and the guys spend every minute they're with me making fun of me, but they won't be joking when they wear the socks I've been making. Warm socks save toes.

"Nothing much."

"How's the painting?"

"Good, actually. Though the color of the kitchen is weird. Who paints a kitchen yellow?"

I chuckle under my breath as I hop into my car and start it. "I'm assuming your mom picked it out?"

"Yeah," he grumps. "My dad isn't too thrilled. He won't say anything, but it's written all over his face. Kind of comical, actually. I'm just glad I don't live here anymore and have to stare at it for hours on end."

"Small victories."

"Damn right."

We're silent for a moment before I ask, "So, did you call just to check in or…?"

The phone rustles before I hear a deep exhale. "No, actually. I-I don't even know how to start this conversation."

"Uh-oh, am I in trouble?"

He snorts. "Not this time, no."

"Then just let it out. I'm freezing my ass off here."

"I feel guilty," he spits out.

I frown and rest my hand on my cold steering wheel. "About what?"

"My sister," he breathes. "She's not doing well, man."

My face pales as I fear the worst. If something happened to her, I don't know what I'd do. We may not be together anymore, and I may not be texting her anymore either, but she still means the world to me. "Did something happen to her?"

"No, no, nothing like that. She—uh—there's no way she's over you. That's my only explanation for the shit-show she's become."

That should make me feel better, but it doesn't. "Did she say something?"

"No, she refuses to talk about it, but she looks like shit. Barely eating. Barely talking. The laughs are limited. She's just not her ever since…well, you know."

"Since we broke up?"

"Yeah."

Well, that makes two of us. I rake a hand down my face. "I don't know what you want me to do about it."

"Text her or something, make her feel better."

"I tried that for months. She doesn't answer them. She doesn't want me to talk to her, Dustin."

There's a long pause, and I almost think he hung up, but he blurts, "Ask her out again."

"What?"

"You heard me. Date my sister."

I shake my head. "It's too late for that, and you know it. The damage is done. Look, I have to go." I don't give him a moment to respond before I hang up, my chest heaving. I could try to ask her back out, but she'll probably say no, and I can't take the heartache all over again. I won't give myself an inch when it comes to hope. I can't. This is me…letting her go.

SIX MONTHS LATER

> **Jacob**
> How's the internship going?

I've been following around the anesthesiologist all day and haven't had a moment to answer the text that came in this morning. Now that it's lunch, though, and I'm on my way to the cafeteria, the time belongs to me.

Me
It's going good. How's campus without everyone in it?

He decided to stay back and take some summer classes this summer. Secretly, I think his new girlfriend is the reason. He didn't want to leave her. Yeah, he finally started dating the girl he met at the beginning of the school year. It took him long enough, and I still haven't met her, but I'm happy for him.

Jacob
It sucks. The parties suck. Classes suck.

Me
But the sex is good.

Jacob
Damn right.

Me
Gym when I get off?

Jacob
Yeah, dude. See ya then.

Smiling, I pocket my phone and glance up but then stop in my tracks. Standing in the hallway is the most beautiful woman I know. Shock takes over for seeing Avery here. She's dressed in green scrubs and hasn't seen me yet, busy talking with another nurse. Did she get an internship at the same hospital as me? Last I heard, she was having a hard time finding one, but here? What are the chances?

I raise my phone and snap a picture of her. There's no way I can't address this. There's no way I can ignore the fast beat of my heart, the way my blood pumps and thumps the inside of my veins.

I glance back up at her and swallow thickly. She laughs at something the other nurse said, but I know her real laugh, and that isn't it.

Gathering the picture into a text message, I send it, along with:

Stunning.

From where I stand, I can hear her phone beep. She picks it up off the counter next to her and opens it up. Her eyes go wide before she starts swiveling around, looking for me. And when she finds me, we just stand there, staring. The nurse beside her starts engaging in a conversation with someone on the other side of the desk, but that doesn't stop Avery from holding my gaze.

God, she's beautiful. Maybe a little tired looking, maybe a little thinner, but she's just as gorgeous as I remember. I can practically smell her unique scent from here, practically hear her silky voice.

I start to walk toward her, my feet moving of their own accord. For a moment, she doesn't move, but then she blinks and bolts. Walking quickly, she heads down the hall, but I'm hot on her heels. I may have given her space, but she's here, and I…I just need to hear her voice. I just need a conversation with her. Anything. I'll take anything.

She practically rips open a door and steps inside. I know what that room is. It's a storage room, and I frown as I approach it. Without thinking, I open the door and step inside. That unique scent swirls around me, and when my eyes land on hers, a weight is lifted off my shoulders.

Tears are streaming down her face before she covers them with shaky fingers and backs up into a stack of totes that come to my waist.

"Avery," I whisper, standing still but wanting to move toward her.

"Don't," she whispers back.

I stand there with her, listening to her sob into her fingers, but I can't stand there long. I'd do anything for this girl, and if she needs comforting, that's exactly what I'm going to give.

Taking the last few steps toward her, I gently grab her wrists and pull them away from her face. Thankfully, she doesn't fight me. Her cheeks are red and shiny from her tears, and her eyelashes are wet.

"Avery, look at me."

"I can't," she groans.

"Why did you run?" I ask after a second.

She shakes her head. "If I would have known you got an internship here, I wouldn't have taken it."

I flex my jaw, her words stinging a bit. "Why?"

"Because!" She throws up her hands, and they slap back at her thighs. "Being around you in last semester's Spanish was torture, Reid. And now you're here..."

"And so are you," I whisper.

"We can't do this."

"We can have this conversation, Avery. We *need* to have this conversation. It's long overdue."

She closes her eyes tight. "I'll quit. I'll tell them I'm not a good fit and try to make something else work. Maybe another program-"

"You're not quitting," I say firmly.

Her eyes snap open. "I can't, Reid. I can't be around you and..."

"And what?" I press quietly.

"And…not touch you. Breathe you in. Share space with you. I can't…I just can't." She sobs once, and fresh tears fall. "You have no idea how hard this is."

"Oh, trust me, I know how hard this is."

"You being here, right now, in the same hospital as me…my heart is breaking all over again. I don't know if I'll survive. I don't even know how to breathe right." She isn't wrong, her breathing is close to hyperventilating.

But despite her current state, my heart sings to the fact that she still wants me. That being here is going to be hard on her because she misses me. "So all those unanswered text messages?"

She crosses her arms and looks away from me again, trying to breathe slowly through her nose. "I didn't want to give us hope. I thought a clean break was important for my brother's-"

"Your brother gave me his blessing a month ago."

Her head whips back to face me. "What?"

I nod and step into her space. Our chests are nearly touching. "I thought you didn't want me, so I didn't tell you."

"I- I-We-I can't—"

I watch as her expression changes, and I try to read every one of her emotions but fail. "There's nothing standing between us anymore," I add, licking my lips. Her eyes zoom to the action. "If you want to…we don't have to be apart anymore, Avery. If that's what you want. Is that what you want, baby girl?"

She tucks her bottom lip in between her teeth as she thinks it over. "We can't just erase the breakup. It's not that simple. We can't just pick up where we left off."

I take a chance and run my knuckles over her cheek, swiping away tears. "Says who?"

She leans into the touch. "I don't know," she answers,

and there's so much honesty in the words that it makes me smile a little. "Society?"

"Screw society. We can do whatever we want. Tell me, Avery. What do you want?"

I watch as her throat bobs on a thick swallow. Her voice is so small when she says, "I want to be me again. You made me feel like me when I was so lost and confused. You brought me back from a dark place in my life and showed me what true happiness could be like. I want that back. I want you, Reid. That's all I want, everything I've wanted for months, and if my brother said -"

It takes everything in me to hold still during her entire speech, but now that she said she wants me back, I take her face in my hands and crush my lips down on hers. I give her all of me. Every last drop, through one kiss. My head spins as I drink her in, inhaling deeply before running my tongue along the seam of her lips, asking for permission. She opens immediately, and I sweep my tongue inside, groaning at the taste of her. A taste I didn't realize I missed until this very moment.

We kiss for what feels like forever, the rest of the world forgotten. There's only us, the equipment surrounding us, and the murmurs of people walking by in the hallway outside the storage room. Her hands around my neck tug at my hair, and my hands move from her face, down her body, and to her hips where I squeeze and pull her tighter against me.

She moans when my erection presses against her core, and I just can't contain myself any longer. Kissing isn't enough. I need more of her, the deepest connection we can have.

"Take off your pants."

"What?" She blinks at me, confused.

"Take them off, Avery," I whisper my command.

Without another word, she does as I ask, and then I'm

lifting her onto the edge of the totes and settling between her thighs. I pull out my cock, rest my forehead against hers, and slide inside of her. She sucks in a breath at the same time that I groan her name.

That familiar tug of her walls sucks on my cock before I start moving. I find her lips again, kissing her more sensually, more lovingly, more meaningful. I swallow every soft mewl she makes and rock my hips against her, picking up my pace until she starts gripping me harder.

"God, I missed you," I murmur against her lips. I grab her shirt and pull it off her body then pull on the hem of mine, slide it off, and fling it to the side.

"I missed you so much, Reid." Her hands start roaming my body, her trailing fingers feeling heavenly on my skin.

I rest my forehead against hers and fuck her with everything I have, slamming into her and knocking the totes into the wall with every pump of my hips. Her breathing picks up pace, and I know she's close. I'm close too—a tingle down the base of my spine—but I won't finish until she does.

"Tell me this is forever," she begs in between pants.

"I'm not going anywhere." I shake my head a little. "I won't let you get away from me again, I can promise you that."

My words do something to her, my promise striking something within her, and then she's tipping her head back, mouth open, as she comes. Her pussy clamps so hard around me that I curse. A few more pumps and I'm following right after her, hands falling beside her as I bend forward a little, my legs weak from the intense orgasm.

Our breathing is in time with each other, but she starts to hiccup a sob. I bend down to capture her gaze, tipping her chin up to meet my eyes. "Sad tears or happy ones?" I ask after a moment.

"Happy," she croaks out.

I smile and press a kiss to her lips before I slide out and go in search of something to clean her up. Once that's done, I toss the cloth in the trash and help her off the totes. We're silent as I hold her hand while she pulls her clothes back on. When we're both finished, she looks up at me, sniffling.

"He really said we could be together?"

I nod. "I can call him and put him on speaker if you want."

She places a hand on my chest. "I believe you. So what do we do now? We just pick up where we left off?"

I gather her in my arms and kiss the top of her head. "Yes. We go back to being Avery and Reid without all the forbidden stuff. We get to kiss out in the open. I get to hold your hand in front of everyone we love. And I get to wrap you in my arms and call you mine for everyone to hear. I love you, Avery. I want a life with you. I want my future to be surrounded by you. I'm not looking to start over. I just want to pretend the last six months, five days, and twelve hours didn't exist."

She snuggles into my chest, gripping my scrubs tightly. "I love you too."

And that's all I need as confirmation. I didn't start out this day—hell, this month—thinking I'd ever get her back, but here she is, in my arms and telling me she loves me. Agreeing to be my girl again. Saying yes to a future with me. I don't know what I did to deserve her, but I'm never, never letting her go. Never.

CHAPTER 31
AVERY MOORE

ONE WEEK LATER

I TRIP over what can only be my pile of shoes by the door in my apartment, Ivy guiding me from behind by the shoulders. She caught me off guard in my room and blindfolded me when my back was turned. Since it's Saturday, we were going to do something, but I had no idea it involved a blindfold.

An hour ago, when she declared that we were going out, she told me to dress nice. I put on the black dress I wore at Dustin's first party and am wearing my hair down, even taking the time to curl it and put on my makeup. I have no idea where we're going, and I have no idea how I'm going to make it down the stairs like this. I tell her as much.

"Spoiler alert," she answers, guiding me into the hall. Our door shuts behind her. "We aren't even leaving the building."

I try to look back at her, but of course, I can't see her. All I see is pitch-black cloth. Where did she even find a blindfold? "What?"

She shimmies me forward until we reach what can only be Dustin's apartment, and she doesn't knock before shuffling us in. I swivel my head around at the soft murmurs.

"We've arrived!" Ivy says cheerfully.

"What's going on?" I ask her. I know there are a bunch of people here. I can practically hear their breathing. I'm proven right when she tiptoes me forward, my heels clacking on the dining room floor until it meets soft carpet and I bump into someone's shoulder.

"Just be patient," she hisses, sitting me down softly on the couch. "And leave the blindfold on."

I feel around the couch to see if I'm the only one on it. I frown when I find out that I really *am* the only one sitting. "Come on, guys. What is this? Dustin? Reid? What the hell is going on?"

Murmurs pick up right before someone places their hand on my knee. I startle when lips land on mine next but then lean into the kiss when I smell that it's Reid. I do blush a little because, even though our relationship is no longer secret, it still feels weird not hiding it.

His lips leave mine, and he leans away. "Take your blindfold off, Avery."

Slowly, I lift it off my head. My eyes take in my surroundings, to all of our friends standing around us, drinks in their hands, and smiles on their faces. Some people have their phones out, recording.

I find Dustin standing with his arm around Ivy, the biggest grin of them all on his face. And when my gaze slides down to Reid, I gasp. My hand flies to my mouth, and my heart skips a beat. He's kneeling before me on one knee, a ring in his hand.

"What are you doing?" I breathe out.

"Avery," he begins, his voice firm and confident. "I met you right here. Caught you, in fact, and from that moment on, I was a goner. All I wanted was you, and then I lost you, and I don't want to ever lose you again. You're it for me, baby girl. You're all I want to wake up to, who I want to fight with, who I want to laugh with. I want to grow old with you. I want to share an epic love that lasts a lifetime. So I'm here tonight, asking you the most important question of my life: Will you marry me?"

The room holds its breath as he waits for my answer. He doesn't have to wait long, however, because I nod and whisper, "Yes. Yes, I'll marry you."

Grinning and surrounded by cheering friends, he takes my hand and slides the ring on my finger. Strong arms wrap around me, and he's pulling me off the couch, picking me up, and spinning me around. Someone starts playing music, and the party begins as his lips find mine and he kisses me the way he always kisses me: as if it'll be his last.

"All right, all right," Dustin says beside us. "Can you put my sister down so I can give her a hug?"

We laugh, and he gently sets me on my feet. I turn to my brother, and he wraps his arms around my neck, squeezing before he says, "Congratulations," in my ear.

"Thank you," I say, squeezing him back.

"I love you, you know that, right?"

I nod. "Love you too."

"We're good?"

"We're good."

And then he releases me because Ivy is whining next to him about it being her turn. I go to her immediately, and we laugh as we hug, rocking back and forth. "This is far better than an evening out," I say to her over the music.

"I thought you might say that," she answers, grinning from ear to ear. She releases me and picks up my hand, eyes wide at the ring. "Jesus, that's huge."

It twinkles under the lights as we both marvel at it. It really is. I've never thought about my dream wedding ring, but Reid has good taste. It makes me wonder if his mom helped him pick it out. I met them just a few days ago, and at first, his mother didn't seem to like me, but as the night went on, she was talking to me like I was a new friend.

"A drink for the soon-to-be bride," Jacob says as he approaches, balancing three drinks in his hand. He passes one to Ivy, then one to me, and keeps the third for himself.

"Thanks," Ivy and I both say together.

A girl slides up beside him and smiles at us. She's stunning with light brown hair that reaches her shoulders and is curled in beach waves, and a pair of blue eyes so blue that they look like ice. "Hello," she greets.

We look questioningly at Jacob before he gets the hint and introduces us. "Guys, this is Jill."

Jill rolls her eyes at the awkward way he said it. "His girlfriend. Honestly, getting him to say that out loud is like cutting a cat's nails."

I laugh and turn my grin to Jacob. "Oh, she's good for you."

"That's what she keeps telling me," he grumbles behind his cup.

"And you know it's true." She turns her attention to me. "I hear you're in the nursing program. I started the program last year. Any tips to get on the professor's good side?"

I cringe. "They don't get along with you?"

A slow grin spreads across her face. "I made the mistake of correcting one last semester and made an enemy out of her. She must have gossiped to her professor friends because now the entire nursing program is giving me the stink eye."

"Oh man, that's rough."

Ivy chuckles. "I like her."

I bump against Ivy's shoulder. "Me too."

She's going to fit in great with the group. I don't know why Jacob hid her for so long. Probably because she terrifies him. But he clearly has feelings for her if he's finally introducing her to us.

I squeal when firm hands grip my shoulders and spin me around. My drink nearly spills out of my cup and onto the carpet as Reid presses me into his chest. He starts to sway us back and forth with the music, and I melt into him. I can't get enough of the way I fit perfectly into him. I don't think that will ever get old.

"No regrets?" he asks in my ear.

I shake my head. "None." And it's the truth. Everything he said in his proposal speech made me want to say it all back to him, to tell him I feel exactly the same way. I'll never regret saying yes to him. He's everything I didn't know I needed and everything that's good for me. My mom keeps reminding me of that fact. She adores him almost as much as I do. But then again, she liked him before we started dating.

Kissing my ear, he murmurs, "I love you, future Avery Rathe."

I pull back and press my lips to his. Our lips slide over each other a few times before I break the kiss and say, "And I love you."

For the rest of my life.

A LOOK AT

DARLING SAVAGE SINS

Dolly never met a red flag she didn't want to fix.

As a therapist, she knows better than to chase the dark, dangerous man watching her from the shadows of the bar. But when Jagger touches her, all mystery and coiled violence, reason doesn't stand a chance. One night in a parking lot becomes an obsession she can't shake. He's every warning sign she's ever ignored, and exactly the kind of broken she's drawn to.

Jagger came back to Ashwood, Oregon for one reason: to save his sister from the Savage Temple cult he barely escaped alive. The brutal compound shaped him into something he can't forgive. A soldier with too many kills on his hands and PTSD that won't let him sleep. He doesn't deserve Dolly's soft hands or her determination to make him whole. But when she inserts herself into his life, refusing to walk away from his darkness, he can't resist the hunt.

Now his father stands between him and his sister's freedom. The law wants him gone. And the deeper Dolly falls into Jagger's world, the more she realizes some souls can't be saved, and some monsters wear the faces of victims. When the final confrontation comes, survival will demand a sacrifice neither of them saw coming.

AVAILABLE APRIL 2026

USA TODAY Bestselling DV Fischer is a mother of two very busy boys, a wife to a wonderful and patient (thank god) husband, an owner of three sock-loving German shorthairs, and slave to a cat they pulled out of a dumpster (literally), Geralt. Together, they live in Sheldon, Iowa.

When DV Fischer isn't chasing after her children, she spends her time typing like a madwoman while consuming vast amounts of caffeine. Just kidding. She can't do that anymore. One cup a day or she regrets all her life choices for the next twenty-four hours.

Known for the darker side of imagination, she enjoys freeing her creativity through plus-size romance that may only exist between the pages, no matter how much we wish otherwise.

www.dvfischer.com

www.ingramcontent.com/pod-product-compliance
Lightning Source LLC
La Vergne TN
LVHW041250110826
845146LV00005BA/1329
* 9 7 9 8 8 9 5 6 7 6 4 5 5 *